THE GERMAN GIRL

THE MONIKA RITTER SERIES
BOOK 1

EOIN DEMPSEY

Copyright © 2024 by Eoin Dempsey

All rights reserved.

No part of this book may be reproduced in any form or by any electronic or mechanical means, including information storage and retrieval systems, without written permission from the author, except for the use of brief quotations in a book review.

This book is for my wife, Jill.

PROLOGUE

Berlin, September 1934

Monika stripped off her receptionist's uniform and removed her clothes from their hangers. She paused to hold the soft, white blouse to her cheek before putting it on. It had been her mother's, and it felt smooth against the skin of her face. Long ago it had carried a faint trace of her mother's perfume, but no more. It had been more than four years, and though Monika tried to keep the memories in her heart, sometimes she felt them slipping away like water through her fingers.

A knock on the staff changing room door jarred her back to the present. She hastily pulled on the blouse. "Don't come in, I'm dressing!"

But the door opened before she finished buttoning up. Herr Aber, the hotel manager, was a bespectacled man in his 40s. "Oh, my apologies, Fraulein..."

Monika grabbed her skirt and held it in front of her to preserve her modesty. "If you don't mind, Herr Aber." She didn't hide the irritation in her voice.

"Of course..." But his eyes lingered on her longer than they should have before he backed out and closed the door.

"I've got to get out of this place," she muttered to herself as she finished getting dressed.

Herr Aber was lurking by the front desk as she emerged into the lobby; she ignored him and hurried out into the street. It was a fine, sunny evening, and she waited for a moment while a group of Hitler Youth singing Nazi songs passed by. Seeing them in the city was unusual, but everything seemed different now. Above her, a Nazi flag hung from a pole above the hotel entrance door. Two years before, it had been the German flag.

After the singing schoolboys had turned the corner, she strolled off in the opposite direction, towards the tram.

Monika had left school a few months before. The lessons had changed so much with the coming of National Socialism that she'd struggled to see the point in staying. There seemed no place for educated women in Hitler's new society, and because of her father's troubles, the money she received for working in the hotel had become essential to the household.

Besides, her feelings about the Nazis had set her apart from almost all her classmates. The simple act of not joining the League of German Girls transformed her into a pariah. All her former friends were members and wore their uniforms with a pride that she couldn't fathom. None of them seemed able to see what was obvious to her. When her father, Gustav Horn, a trade union leader, was arrested, the Nazis dismissed it as a mistake that was quickly rectified when the Gestapo released him days later. Those three days he had been gone had been the worst of Monika's life. She had been just 15 at the time and completely alone. Those horrific days sparked a hatred of the Nazis in her heart that still burned there.

Yet her father had been one of the lucky ones. Most of his friends and former colleagues had disappeared a few short weeks after the Nazis had come to power; destroying the trade unions was one of their top priorities.

Most of these men were still being held in the shadowy prison camps set up by the government, which officially didn't exist. Her former friends wrote them off as enemies of the state who threatened every loyal German. The Nazis could do little wrong in the eyes of her former friends. The only person who seemed to share her opinions was her beloved cousin, Sarah, in the faraway city of Ulm, but Sarah's father was a card-carrying party member and forbade her from speaking out.

It was almost six o'clock when Monika arrived back at the apartment she shared with her father.

Gustav was sitting by the window with a cigarette in his hand, staring out at the fading day. He held a framed photo of Monika's mother in his hand—the only one they had of her. Several beer bottles sat on the table beside him, most of them empty.

"There's my girl," he said, looking up with a lop-sided smile. He was tall and still handsome, though his blond hair was thinning and his ordinarily clean-shaven face was thick with stubble. He set the photo down amongst the beer bottles. "How was work?"

She resisted the temptation to tell him about her lascivious boss. She could handle him herself and didn't want to trouble her father. "It was fine. The usual. How was your job?" He had found work in a factory making door hinges at a fraction of what the trade union had paid him. It was the best he could do.

He shook his head in answer to the question. "The conditions are dreadful. Without a strong union to represent them, the workers are powerless in the face of the Nazis and their fat-cat owner friends."

He opened up another bottle and drank some more.

Monika stood looking at him as he settled back in the armchair and stared out the window once more. She feared for him. He seemed lost without the men of his union. Without standing for them, it seemed he had little to strive for. He had always been a committed father, but even she didn't need him as much as she once had. Gustav Horn was a man who needed a cause to fight for, and the Nazis had robbed him of that.

"I'll see to dinner," she said after a short silence, and when he didn't answer, she walked into the kitchen. She wasn't much of a cook but was superior to her father and had assumed dinner duties after her mother had died; today, she'd make schnitzel and potatoes.

Half an hour later, at the dining table, her father rested his hand on hers for a second before they began eating. "Thank you for this. I don't know what I'd do without you."

She returned his smile but didn't speak.

He lifted his fork and poked at his food before setting the fork back down. "I'm so sorry this is happening to you," he said.

She lowered her knife. "What do you mean?" But she suspected she knew what was coming; he said it so often.

He was shaking his head sadly. "You're 16. No one should have to deal with what this country has become at your age. I can hardly process it myself. The way they've indoctrinated Germany's youth…. it's repulsive."

"You know I'm not part of that."

"Even so, everyone you know is. All I want for you is a chance for you to shine. You're so smart, so determined. Just like your mother."

Monika felt tears welling in her eyes but fought them back. "Eat, Dad," she said. "Your food is getting cold."

"The Nazis are animals. Monsters. I think about my former colleagues in those prison camps all the time." He forked some potato into his mouth, then dropped his cutlery again and sat back on the chair. "Sometimes, I think we should get out of Berlin."

"And go where? To Ulm?" Monika loved the city and the surrounding area where her cousin lived.

"Somewhere we can escape the Nazis. Ulm isn't far enough."

His beer was empty, so he got up to fetch another. He never used to drink during the week but now seemed to all the time.

As he sat down opposite her again, he said, "I didn't realize it at the time, but it was perfect. What we had was everything I ever wanted. I had the two most beautiful girls in the world, and my men, who needed me. I got so caught up in everyday problems that I missed it. I never saw that I had everything a man could ever need."

Monika pushed her plate forward. Finding the words wasn't easy. "We still have each other."

He reached forward and took her hand. "You're all that matters to me now, Monika. You're my reason for everything."

He was also hers, but the words caught in her throat for some reason. "What are we going to do, Dad?" she asked instead.

"I don't know, my darling, but you deserve better."

"Well, at least eat what I've cooked for you," she smiled at him.

When he'd done as she asked, she cleared the plates and carried them to the kitchen.

Her father was sitting back at the window when she returned, listening to classical music on the radio. He preferred jazz, but jazz was anathema to the Nazis due to the skin color of most of those who played it, so classical was all there was unless you wanted to run the risk of listening to the forbidden foreign radio stations. She settled down in the chair opposite him with a book, one of the few that hadn't been banned. After finishing another bottle, her father stopped drinking. She didn't know if it was a conscious decision or if he ran out. Either way, she was glad.

It was after ten o'clock when she rose from her chair to go to bed. "Good night, Dad." She walked over and put her hand on his shoulder.

"Good night, my sweet." He looked up with his crooked smile and blurry eyes.

A thumping on the front door jarred Monika awake. She sat up in bed, her eyes heavy with tiredness. It was still pitch-black outside. The banging thundered again, and a cold trickle of fear slid down her spine. She got out of bed and felt for her dressing gown. An almighty crash followed. Men were shouting. In the living room, she could hear her father yelling in a frightened voice, "What's this about?"

Cautiously, she opened her bedroom door.

Two men in plain clothes stood flanked by six SA members in their familiar brown uniforms. They were shining their flashlights into her father's face. He was on his feet, shielding his eyes.

"Gustav Horn, come with us," one of the two Gestapo men said.

"What's the charge?"

"I am Kriminalkommissar Posche. We have a warrant for your arrest. This can be as hard or as easy as you make it," the man responded, and three of the SA men grabbed him.

For a moment, Monika stood alone, utterly helpless, as her father struggled to break free. A punch to the jaw slowed him down, and the men dragged him through the broken front door, kicking and yelling. Before she knew it, she had run forward and was pulling at their arms with tears rolling down her cheeks.

"Get off him!" she screamed.

One of the men shoved her back. "Your father is an enemy of the state and will be taken for re-education!"

She staggered and fell against the wall, then ran after them again. "Where are you taking him?" she roared.

One of the plainclothes Gestapo men stood barring her exit as, behind him, the others threw her father in the back of a police truck. "You can expect a letter in due course," he said coldly before taking his place in the passenger seat.

Unable to believe what was happening, she ran after the truck, trying to steal a last glimpse of her father as they took him away, but she saw only the black morass of the inside of the truck. It sped away, and in seconds, the street was quiet again. It was all over. She broke down, collapsing to her knees, hot tears running down her face.

The letter the Gestapo agent promised came a few weeks later, explaining that her father had been detained indefinitely and could not receive visitors. Three months after that, another official letter arrived. It was simple, with only a few lines to explain that her father had died and his body had already been disposed of. There would be no funeral, no chance to say goodbye.

She was completely alone.

1

New York City, March 1942.

Monika Ritter still dreamed of her past. She was in America now, and though she had been here for almost three years, she still felt like a stranger in a strange land. She hadn't seen Germany since 1936, when she and her now husband, Michael, had fled the country with his sister, Maureen.

Thoughts of that awful time when Maureen and Michael had saved her from the Nazi guard's lecherous advances came when she was alone in the dark. She could still feel his rough hands on her as he threw her down on the ground. She could still smell the foul scent of his breath and feel his weight on top of her. The sound of the gunshot that almost killed Michael when he and his sister came upon the scene still rang in her ears.

Monika felt no regret for Maureen killing that man or any of the actions she or her friends took that night when they helped the starving gypsy family escape from the camp. It had been a turning point in her life—a hinge that had first led her to Paris and then to marry Michael and move with him to America, a country she knew little about before stepping off the boat here. Michael had done his best to prepare her, of course. He'd talked to her for hours about what life would be like in New York, but his words, honest as they were, had done little to ready her to live in a country where she didn't speak the language and which was now at war with the land of her birth.

Michael stirred beside her. It was almost four in the morning, but she'd slept little. Monika wanted to wake her husband and tell him that the weight of living here was too much for her. She wanted to tell him that she couldn't take the shocked looks on people's faces when they heard the accent she tried to hide every day of her life. She wanted to find a place where the war didn't exist, where people didn't see her as an enemy amongst them, where she could be another face in the crowd and live as everyone else seemed to.

Instead, she got out of bed and went to the window. A car rumbled past on the street below. She'd been in this apartment with Michael for almost a year now. As a Berliner, she was used to the hustle and bustle of the big city. That didn't bother her. But something else did. Something was missing. The hole inside her was growing by the day and was becoming harder to hide from her husband. There were only so many times she could shrug off his concerns. But what was there to say? It wasn't as if he could actually do anything to help her. No one could. Some burdens couldn't be shed. She was trying to accept hers without it crushing her entire life under its weight.

She pressed her forehead against the cool glass of the window and peered down at the empty street three stories below her. She tried to picture it as if it were in Berlin. The government didn't erect flags in its own honor on every street here. The sickness that had infected Germany hadn't yet spread to America. No one in the bars and restaurants of Manhattan thought a Nazi invasion was imminent, and all were thankful that the vastness of the ocean between the eastern seaboard and the shores of war-torn Europe would protect them from the seemingly unstoppable force of the German army.

Still, the city was a different place since the attack on Pearl Harbor the previous December. The dithering of a largely immigrant population, which wanted to wash its hands of a conflict it saw as an old world problem, had been brushed aside. The populace rallied to the cause and, with President Roosevelt's approval, moved from a stance of isolationism to one of war almost overnight. Within days of the attack, tens of thousands of New Yorkers had lined up outside overwhelmed recruiting offices to volunteer to fight back. The Port of New York had been transformed into a staging point to feed and support the war efforts of both the British and their embattled Soviet counterparts and soon would begin sending American troops by the thousands.

Monika was glad the American war effort was underway at last, yet she worried it was too late. Every day, she read the papers with gritted teeth as they detailed story after story of Nazi successes. It seemed the Wehrmacht was unstoppable. The British were on their knees, and the American army was clearly a pitiful product of years of isolationism and neglect. The Nazis were the bullies in the international schoolyard doing whatever took their fancy.

It was so hard for her to find a role in it all. It was impossible to be accepted when everyone she met thought she was one of *them* because she was so obviously German. She was fluent in English—it had only taken her about six months; her mother had always told her she had a flair for languages. But the thick accent she still couldn't shake singled her out for angry looks.

At least she hadn't been treated as the Japanese had over on the West Coast. Thousands had already been removed from their homes, and a special internment camp had been set up in

California to house ten thousand Japanese Americans deemed as a threat to national security. It frightened her and made her think of the early days of the concentration camps in Germany. She had only been a child then and, like most of the population, knew little of their existence at first. But all that changed in September 1934 when the Gestapo took her father away for the crime of being a trade union leader.

Standing at the window, she closed her eyes to stave off the avalanche of pain that always came with the thoughts of her father. She felt a tear run down her cheek and wiped it away, ashamed to cry, even alone. The day her father was taken away, she had collapsed weeping in the street. But then she had come to a decision. She would survive, carry on, keep her feelings hidden, and never show emotion in public again.

She turned back to the bed. Michael still hadn't moved. The only sound in the dark room was that of his gentle breathing. She climbed back under the covers beside him and put her arms around him. He uttered a few gentle protestations, but she held on. He wriggled a little but was asleep again in seconds.

She shut her eyes, trying to quiet her mind with images of tranquil country days drenched in lazy sunshine, dredging for happy memories of her youth and days at the lake with her parents or visiting her cousin in the countryside. Her mother's face was becoming hazier with each passing year. It had been ten years since she'd died, and Monika had no photographs to remind her or show Michael how much she looked like her. They'd left Berlin in such a hurry that Monika hadn't time to take anything, not even that one framed image of her mother. She'd left everything behind. No one had known her parents here. It was as if her past didn't exist. Michael said he was happy to talk about her childhood, but he didn't know any of the people in the stories, so he couldn't picture it with her. It wasn't his fault. None of this was.

Frustration burned through her entire body as she let her hands slide from Michael's body. Her husband seemed glad to be free from her grip and rolled away in his sleep. She lay on her back and stared up at the dark ceiling. She told herself how painful everything could seem in the loneliness of a sleepless night, but the fire in her heart burned on.

Michael was already at the breakfast table when she emerged from the bedroom in her dressing gown. It was a Saturday, so he hadn't had to rush off for work. He greeted her with a smile, looking up from his newspaper. "I wasn't expecting you to sleep in so long. Your breakfast has gone a bit cold."

"That's all right. Thank you for making it." She sat at the table and helped herself to the scrambled eggs with sausage he had prepared.

"Bill Smithers joined up yesterday," Michael said as she forked the lukewarm eggs into her mouth. "The Army."

"Did he?" She lowered her eyes. This wasn't the first time her husband had broached this conversation, and it was hard to know what to say. She knew the importance of what was happening in the world more than most and didn't want to hold him back from what he saw as his duty, but what would she be here without him?

"Most of the men under 30 have gone from the firm now, and some of the older men too. Bill is ten years older than I am. Has a wife and three kids at home too."

Michael was 24, and while he wasn't in the peak physical shape he'd been in when he competed at the Olympics in '36, he was fitter than most.

He pushed the newspaper across to her. The headline on the front page was about the possibility of American troops landing in North Africa to join the fight there. "Stalin's begging

Roosevelt and Churchill to engage the Germans in North Africa on a large scale to relieve pressure on the Eastern Front. The Russians are getting pummeled."

"I'm surprised they've lasted this long."

"So is Hitler. He didn't expect the war of attrition it's turned into out there. His tanks are running out of fuel. They need to take the oilfields in the South Caucasus before they can push on." He folded the newspaper and put it down. The silence between them swelled, enveloping them both.

She tried to concentrate on her food for a few more seconds but then blurted her fears. "You want to join up, don't you?"

Michael hesitated before answering. He put down his cup of coffee. Rationing hadn't begun yet, but rumor had it that it wasn't far down the pipeline. "How long do you think we'll be able to sit here, eat eggs, and drink coffee?" He tried to smile, but it came as a pained expression.

"Answer the question," she shot back. "What do you want?"

"I saw so many things in my time in Berlin. So many awful things." He looked at her with pity. "I haven't experienced the level of suffering you have. I spent less than four years in Germany, but you were born and raised there. The Nazis destroyed your life. My experience doesn't compare."

She reached across the narrow table and cupped his cheek. "I'd probably be dead or in a concentration camp if it wasn't for you. Remember what my intentions were when we met? I was willing to do anything to get to Goebbels, just so I could try to kill him. My life would be over now if I hadn't fallen in love with you."

He placed his hand over hers. "That doesn't mean I don't feel responsible for you. I brought you here, away from your friends and the few remaining family members you had. I took you from the life you knew."

"Our time in New York hasn't been perfect, but I can only imagine what living in Berlin is like these days. We'd be underground if we were there. The entire population must be living in fear."

"Those that aren't should be."

"What I'm saying is that you don't need to feel responsible for me—not here. I'm free—if not from people's perceptions of me, from the tentacles of the government, at least. And that's far more important. I don't blame the average person on the street for flinching when they hear my accent."

"They're ignorant and rude!"

"They're normal people. They consume what the newspapers and the newsreels tell them. They see the baying crowds at Hitler's rallies. It's all too easy to forget about the rest of the German people and their feelings toward the Nazi regime."

"How many Germans are displeased with Hitler and his war, do you think?"

"No one knows. How is anyone meant to speak out in a country where you can be sent to jail for making jokes about the Führer? Can you imagine if that were the case here, and people were jailed for making fun of Roosevelt?"

He smiled weakly. "The police would have to raid every bar on Friday and Saturday night each week. It'd be like prohibition all over again, except this time for making jokes."

The sun broke through the clouds, and golden light poured in through the windows behind him, illuminating everything around them. He was still as handsome as the night she'd met him before the games in '36. How could she bear to lose him?

"You still haven't answered the question. What do you want, Michael?"

Her husband clasped his hands together and leaned forward, more forthright than before. "I want to serve my country. I want to do my part to rid the world of the Nazi evil I saw. I can't do nothing. I might not have a choice, anyway. Thousands are being drafted all over America. If it wasn't for you...." His voice trailed off as if the following words were too much to utter.

"What?" Monika asked. "What would you have done if it wasn't for me?"

"I would have joined up already," he said bluntly.

"I'm sorry to have held back your ambitions." The hurt she felt from his words wasn't anything new. The sense of loss and abandonment was something she'd carried with her since her mother died. Some days she hid it better than others, but it was always there.

"It's not like that," he said, sounding repentant but also excited. His desire to fight was plain to see in his eyes.

A deep feeling of frustration coursed through her body. She brought her hands to cover her face before removing them to speak again. "I don't want you to leave me."

"And I don't want to leave you. But thousands of couples around the country are having this same conversation as we speak."

"Thousands of men are speaking to their German wives about enlisting? Thousands of would-be soldiers are leaving behind their spouses who've already lost everything to the Nazis? And why should you be the one to fight them? If either of us have earned that right, shouldn't it be me?"

"You can do your part. You could work at the harbor or one of the factories producing weapons. Women doing the jobs the men no longer can."

"You think they would give me a job in a munitions factory, with my German accent?"

He sat back with his hands on his head, his eyes fixed on the wall behind her. Apparently, he had no answer to her question.

After a few tense seconds, she asked, "What's your plan? When are you going to enlist? Army or Navy?"

"I was thinking about joining the Air Force."

She felt sick and envious at the same time. "To fly planes? What do you know about flying?"

"I've always dreamed of it. I think I'd like to try it out. I might not get a choice if I don't enlist before I get drafted."

"And I'll be here, doing nothing…" She got out of her seat. It all felt like too much. She went to the window once more. In her mind, planes were being shot out of the air and plummeting to the ground. She would much rather face that danger instead of him.

"Bomber or fighters?" she asked, trying to sound calm.

"I don't know yet. I'll go where I'm sent." He put his arms around her from behind, nuzzling his face into her shoulder. "I can't stand the thought of leaving you," he said.

Monika knew it was no use. The argument was over. "Just make sure you come back to me." She tried to keep her voice light. "I don't want to live alone in a foreign country that hates me."

"No one hates you. No one who's ever known you has hated you."

"This place isn't mine. Perhaps it will be someday, but not while this war continues."

They stood silently at the window for a few seconds, staring at the people and traffic below. She tried to think of something happier to say. "Do we still have that dinner with Lisa and your father tonight?"

"Yes. In the Plaza Hotel. It's a chance for you to dress up."

She smiled awkwardly. "It doesn't seem right dressing up when so many around the world are suffering."

"It's to buy war bonds."

"Still." Unable to maintain her pretense of cool detachment, she unwound her husband's arms from around her and retreated to the bedroom, leaving Michael standing at the window.

As she sat on the bed with her head in her hands, wishing

for something worthwhile to do, she suddenly felt the presence of her mother so strongly that she thought if she opened her eyes, she would see her. But when she did, there was no one there.

When Michael came to the door a few seconds later, she asked him to leave her alone. She didn't want him to see her cry.

2

The sun set over the city as Monika changed into her black sequined evening dress. It was a few years old, but it still fit her as well as it did the day she bought it. As Michael changed into his tuxedo behind her, she sat in front of the dresser to brush her auburn hair.

She wasn't looking forward to dinner. Michael's father, a man who'd gone from rags to riches and then back again, had developed a taste for nights such as these during his time as an arms manufacturer in Berlin in the 30s. But formal events reminded Monika too much of the time after her father was taken, when she had to do whatever it took to survive. She'd taken advantage of the fact that older men were willing to buy her things in exchange for a dance or sometimes more. It wasn't something she would ever boast about, but it wasn't a time she was ashamed of either. She'd survived alone with little help other than what her aunt and uncle could afford to give her before Michael came along.

Her husband never made the mistake of claiming that he'd rescued her. Instead, they both recognized that they'd saved one another. She'd met Michael when she was out with one of those lonely rich men. She always went for a certain type, and Erich Miner, the man she'd been out with the night she met Michael, was a perfect mark. He was a widower for less than a year, and she saw immediately that all he wanted was his wife back. The lure of a pretty girl less than half his age was nothing to him in comparison to that.

Monika had acquired skills when she'd been a professional dance partner to older men at the Hotel Adlon in Berlin for the year she worked there. She could read people, could see in their eyes the truths they were trying to hide. It was a survival technique some of the older girls had alerted her to. It wasn't something that could be taught, but they'd help her recognize the abilities dormant within her. Too many girls had suffered beatings or worse at the hands of pathetic, frustrated men. She'd been determined not to let that happen to her and, for the most part, had played it safe. She'd made enough money to get by, rarely thinking about what was to come next. Her life had been a series of false interactions—pretending to be charmed by men she wished deep down she'd never met.

Monika often wondered how she'd been able to fall for Michael or anyone else after she'd closed her heart to emotion for so long. She'd once thought of love as a commodity to be bought and sold, yet the recent decisions she'd made in her life had been steered by it – abandoning her suicidal plan to assassinate Goebbels and coming here to this land where she was the enemy. Her heart had led her to this New York City apartment and the man changing into his tuxedo behind her. Who was now preparing to abandon her, putting his country over his love for her – or that's how it felt.

Michael was waiting for her in the living room as she emerged from the bedroom in her finery. He applauded and wolf-whistled.

"Oh, knock it off," she said, amused.

"You're getting the American phrases down now," he said in German.

"Speak English to me," she said. She almost always spoke English now. She saw her native language as her past and English as her future. Sometimes, she dared to wonder whether she'd return to Berlin one day, but it was a question she had no answer to. It would be impossible unless Hitler and his National Socialists were wrested from power.

Michael held the door for her as they left the apartment. "Did I tell you how beautiful you look tonight?" he asked as they walked to the stairwell.

"I figured it out with the whistling," she said. "You look wonderful too, my dear."

He took her hand as they passed through the lobby. People at their mailboxes stood back to watch them pass; they made a beautiful couple.

In the street, Michael flagged down a taxi, and then it was a ten-minute ride to the Plaza, situated at the southeast corner of Central Park. Her husband stepped out first and held the door for her. "Lisa and my father said they'd meet us inside," he smiled.

She tucked her arm into his, wondering how many more times they'd get to do something like this before he enlisted. Perhaps this was the last.

"I'm planning to enjoy this," she said to him as they ascended the stairs, and despite her earlier misgivings, it was true. She had decided to savor every moment with him.

Michael answered her with another smile. "You should. The cream of New York is here."

"It's an amazing hotel. Look at all the marble. How did your father get invited to an event like this? This isn't Berlin five years ago. He isn't the captain of industry here that he was over there."

Michael's father, Seamus Ritter, had been forced to leave his factories and his mansion behind when he fled Germany just before the war began in 1939. He was just an investment manager for a local bank in New York now — far less rich and powerful than he'd been in Berlin.

"I think an old friend of his is in town."

"Who?"

"A man called Bill Hayden. He wouldn't tell me exactly who he was, just that he knew him from his time in Berlin. He worked at the American Embassy there before the Nazis shut it down when Hitler declared war."

"Sounds mysterious. I wonder what the connection is?"

"Who knows? We live in mysterious times, my darling."

The doorman greeted them with a tip of his hat and directed them to the Rose Room, a magnificent ballroom with tapestries draped on the walls and pillars painted gold extending 40 feet up to a rounded ceiling. A man in a tuxedo carrying a silver platter offered them a glass of champagne as they entered, which they both accepted with thanks. The 18-strong band at the edge of the dance floor was playing livelier music than she had expected, and the floor was almost full of couples jitterbugging. Realization dawned on her, and she grabbed her husband by the arm. "That's the Glenn Miller Orchestra!"

"Surprise!" he winked. "I wasn't going to tell you—it's not just a dinner."

"I can't believe it!"

She looked around for her father-in-law and his wife. All the men were dressed exactly alike. The women wore an array of brightly colored dresses. It was just as it had been when she'd been paid to dance with men at events like this. It was all so familiar, and despite her excitement over the band, her determination to enjoy herself faltered; she gripped onto Michael's arm.

A voice from the bar called Michael's name, and there was

Seamus Ritter with Lisa, Michael's stepmother, both with glasses of champagne. The couple had been married for almost ten years and had met soon after Seamus arrived in Berlin in the late months of '32—just a few weeks before Hitler became Chancellor of Germany, and everything was turned on its head.

Seamus put down his glass and greeted them with a warm embrace. "This brings back a few memories, doesn't it?" he said.

Monika wanted to say that not all memories were good but kept her sentiments to herself as she kissed Lisa on the cheek. "Beautiful venue," she murmured.

"Yes, we were just wondering, what are you doing here, Father?" Michael grinned. "The average person in this room probably spends more on ivory backscratchers than I earn in a year. And no offense, but you're not the man you used to be in that regard."

"I'm well aware," Seamus replied. "Money was always like water between my fingers, anyway. I'm just happy with what I've got these days." He put his arm around Lisa's shoulders.

"Then how...?"

"Like I said, my old friend Bill from Berlin called me at work last week. He said he had four tickets to spare and asked me to come and bring the two of you. I don't know if he's here, though..." His eyes searched the crowd.

Lisa linked Monika's arm and pulled her aside, speaking to her in English. Lisa often used German in private, but in public, she abandoned her native tongue in case anyone was listening in.

"How are you?" she asked sympathetically.

Monika answered with a cool shrug of her shoulders. "Michael is planning to enlist."

"Ah... He told you then."

"Just this morning. Am I the last person to know?"

"We've all known this has been coming for a while. You included. Don't fool yourself, Monika."

Monika nodded, keeping her face neutral, as always, hiding the depth of her pain. "I suppose I did."

"Are you very worried about being here without him, as a German?"

Monika forced a smile. "I'll just keep my mouth shut wherever I go."

Lisa laughed and squeezed her arm. "Brave girl. I know the feeling. Ironically, I'm only comfortable around Germans even though I had to flee the country!"

Before Monika could answer, her father-in-law took Lisa by the hand. "I'm sorry to interrupt, but I must ask this beautiful lady to dance."

Monika finished her drink and put down the glass as the older couple walked out onto the dance floor. "Well, Michael. Are you going to ask me to dance?"

"I thought you'd never ask." Smiling, he led her onto the dance floor and held her close as they swept around. "You know, I've been thinking," he said, his cheek to hers. "Maybe there are other ways you can be a part of this. You could apply to be a nurse or join the administrative corps. Surely they'd see how valuable you could be."

Monika leaned back in his arms, looking at him for a long two seconds. Neither prospect he mentioned was an enticing one. He would get to choose exactly what he wanted to do to aid the war effort. Why couldn't she fly planes? But she kept her thoughts to herself. Michael wasn't going to be able to solve this problem. It was the way things were. And, of course, it was honorable to be a nurse or a secretary. Every little bit helped, now that America had joined the war. It was just… Well, it felt so *little*. Even if she was allowed to do it, which she doubted.

Suppressing her rebellious thoughts, she closed her eyes

and let the music take her away. This might be one of their last nights together, and she wasn't about to waste it.

The song ended, and Glenn Miller himself came to the microphone to announce dinner, after reminding the patrons of what they were there to do—buy war bonds. The white-clothed tables set around the dance floor were laid with silver cutlery, crystal glasses, and flowers. They found their seats beside Michael's father, stepmother, and two other men, whom Seamus Ritter introduced as Arnold Swain and Terry Plimpton. They were both investment bankers.

Moments later, uniformed waiters descended with silver platters and bottles of red wine.

Once everyone had been served, Monika took care to savor each bite of the tender beef. It seemed to melt in her mouth.

"You won't get many meals like this in the Army Air Forces," she murmured to her husband.

"Don't I know it?" he grinned back, forking some more sauteed potatoes into his mouth.

Between courses, the sound of a fork on the side of a glass caught the crowd's attention. A man in uniform stepped up to the stage, and Michael's father beamed. "There he is," he said with satisfaction. "I was wondering when he was going to turn up."

"Who is he?" Lisa asked, as Monika listened in, intrigued.

Seamus looked a little evasive. "Bill Hayden. I knew him during the Great War. We fought together in France."

Monika turned her eyes back towards the stage, wondering. Hayden was a handsome man in his late 40s with thinning hair. He coughed before taking the microphone.

"Hello folks, my name is Colonel William Hayden of the United States Army. Thank you for coming here tonight. You all know what we're here to do."

A few people applauded before he cut them off, gesturing with his arm towards the wings as three glamorous young women dressed in factory clothes emerged onto the stage holding up a massive poster set on a rigid cardboard background of a woman working in the factories. Three other men dressed as pilots followed, carrying another poster of a handsome young pilot sitting in a cockpit, giving the thumbs up. Hayden turned back to his audience.

"I don't need to remind you what desperate times we're living in. Hitler and his armies have run riot in Europe and are pushing further east every day. Even the President himself is wondering how long our allies in Russia can hold out against the Nazi onslaught. And in the oceans of the world, Hitler's wolf packs are giving our poor sailors a pasting. Make no mistake, ladies and gentlemen, our children's and grandchildren's futures will be decided by the actions we take today. The Nazis are an enemy the likes of which none of us have ever known. I was in Berlin for years in the 30s. I saw their savagery and madness first-hand. And now they're inflicting the same horrors they unleashed on Kristallnacht on innocent civilians all over Europe. Who among us hasn't seen the newsreels depicting Nazi cruelty?"

He paused and looked at the hushed crowd for a few seconds before continuing. "Hitler and the Nazis will not stop until they have conquered the civilized world. I know from meeting the man myself that his ambition is limitless. The calls for isolationism and not getting involved in what some called "a foreign war" were music to his ears, for he knows that if we come together and commit to the fight, he won't beat us. I, like some others in this room, was in France in 1918. As savage as that war was and as great as the losses we suffered were, the conflict we find ourselves in today is far greater, far more terrible, and will require more sacrifice than we ever thought possible. The simple truth of the matter is that the United State Armed Forces are years behind those of the Nazis. While we spent our time hiding our heads in the sand in the last decade, the Nazis were building their armies, investing unprecedented sums in their existing army and navy while spending billions on research and development. As a result, we find ourselves facing the most technologically advanced fighting force in the world, and what do we have? I've seen our men train with rifles older than I am, with planes and tanks so outdated as to be rendered obsolete. These are the machines that your sons and grandsons will be relying on to save their lives when we come face to face with the might of the SS and the Wehrmacht."

Monika turned to Michael. He was already looking at her. She gripped his hand as they both turned back to face Hayden.

"I, like many of you here, am getting too old to fight on the front lines in this war of wars. And also, like many here, I have spent my fair share of time in the mud. But as every great patriot knows, service to our country doesn't end as our hair thins, and our knees start to hurt." Some people in the crowd laughed. "There are a thousand ways to support our nation and the democratic way of life we all cherish in their time of greatest need."

Again, he gestured towards the posters of the female factory worker and the male pilot being held up behind him.

"We have the workforce and the facilities to produce the machinery to turn this war around. We have everything we need at our disposal to send a message to Hitler and his evil cronies that we will not lie down! And that when Hitler declared war on these United States, he was signing the death warrant of his evil regime!" The crowd cheered. Several men rose to their feet to clap their hands.

"President Roosevelt has mobilized the government to change our society to what it will need to be in order to defeat our nefarious enemy. The tax system is changing. The industrial system is changing. We all have to change!" More cheers followed, but Hayden wasn't finished yet. "I saw with my own eyes what Hitler did to Germany. He transformed it from a failing nation into a military superpower in six years. We must do the same, except in six months. So, open your pocketbooks, ladies and gentlemen. There's no risk. Every bond you buy today is backed by the United States government and will pay interest over time on your investment. But this is about more than money. This is about securing our freedom and the democratic way of life for future generations. Each one of the people behind me is a real pilot or factory worker, and they'll be coming around to each table to take orders for the war bonds that will build the tanks and planes we need to defeat the Nazis."

"Very clever, Bill," Seamus Ritter said, smiling to himself. "No one's going to say no to a pilot or a factory worker."

"Give generously," Hayden urged. "You wouldn't be here if you couldn't afford it. Make sure you can look yourself in the eye next time you stand in front of the mirror, knowing you did all you could to keep our boys on the front lines safe."

Hayden stepped off the stage as the three male pilots and three female factory workers started doing the rounds with notebooks in their hands.

Every fat cat they approached attempted to outdo the last with their acts of patriotic generosity, and Monika admired Hayden's tactics while dreading being asked herself.

"That was quite the speech," Plimpton said, turning to Seamus. "You know that officer?"

"I used to. We ran into each other in Berlin a few years ago. Good man."

"I'll say," Plimpton replied, getting out his pocketbook. "Now, let's see what we can do for our boys."

Soon, one of the factory workers, a beautiful young girl with bright blue eyes and shining blonde hair, arrived at their table. She went to Arnold Swain first. Speaking loudly, she marked him down for $50,000 worth. Monika watched as Seamus Ritter pulled awkwardly at his collar, flushing from the neck up. Once, her father-in-law would have been able to afford a similar amount, but no longer. He'd been an arms manufacturer during the gold rush of Nazi military expansion, but that was before the war. He'd left his mansion back in Berlin and spent his money on helping his Jewish workers escape.

"I think I might have been invited to the wrong event," he murmured with an embarrassed smile as the girl approached him. Lisa put her hand over her husband's, leaning across him. "We're not in the position to give as much as some here," she said softly to the girl. How about $500?"

The young woman glared at them as she heard Lisa's German accent before taking the order with cursory thanks and moving on to Michael.

"We'll take the same amount," Monika said before Michael could speak. She knew they could hardly afford $100, but although she could see Lisa trying to put on a brave face, the woman's thin-lipped smile told of her shame at being considered reluctant to give or being "on the wrong side" because of her accent.

Michael intervened. "I'm sorry, we can't afford that. Put us down for $200."

The factory worker looked at him in disgust, as if he'd just suggested she pay him the money, and then glared at Monika as if she thought it was all her fault for being German.

"My husband is signing up for the Army Air Forces," Monika said to the girl, but she had already moved on to Mr. Plimpton and his wife, who also pledged $50,000.

Michael turned to his father, flushed with humiliation. "Why did your friend Hayden waste four tickets on us? He must know we're not in this league, so what was the point?"

"Knowing him, I'm sure he had his reasons," Seamus said uncomfortably, squeezing his wife's hand with an apologetic glance as the factory worker moved on to fairer pastures.

The waiters brought peach cobbler and fresh cream for dessert and placed a plate in front of each person at the table at the same time.

Monika was thankful for the distraction the dessert offered. She tried to convince herself that the other people at the table hadn't overheard how little they had to give, but she couldn't shake the feeling of being despised.

After finishing her peach cobbler, she lit a cigarette and sat back in the chair while the others talked.

The band began again after the plates were cleared, and people began drifting out onto the dance floor. The factory workers and pilots were still working the room. Somehow, Monika doubted what Hayden had said about them being genuine. They seemed far too glamorous to be ordinary factory girls and military men.

"I'm going to the bar," she said to Michael and stood up without waiting for an answer.

He joined her while she was still waiting to be served.

"You think it's uncouth in this company if I order a beer?" she asked.

"Do, and I'll join you."

The bartender poured two beers from bottles and pushed them over the counter. Michael handed one to his wife and toasted the war effort. Monika clinked his glass and tried to smile; the thought of losing him was agony.

A voice called, "Michael!" It was Bill Hayden, with Seamus and Lisa. He shook Michael's hand and smiled inquisitively at Monika while Seamus introduced her.

"I don't believe you've met Michael's Berliner wife, Monika…"

"It's a pleasure," Hayden shook her hand.

"By the way, are you really a colonel now?" Seamus asked as Hayden leaned across him to signal to the bartender.

The tall man shot him a sideways smile. "Mm…that was a

bit of self-promotion, I must admit. I wasn't even meant to be giving the speech. Colonel Arbuckle got food poisoning, and I had to step in." He ran his hands along the sleeves of the uniform he was wearing. "Fits nicely, doesn't it?"

Seamus laughed and shook his head. "Always with the smoke and mirrors."

"As long as the people buy war bonds. Everything else is just details."

"We were asking the question at the table why you invited us here," Lisa said.

"We're not in danger of straining our backs picking up our wallets, she means," Seamus said.

"Can't I invite my old war buddy for a nice evening in the city?" Hayden answered with a smile as he got the bartender's attention. "That beer looks good," he said. "I'll take one of them. One for you, Seamus? Lisa, champagne?" Once he'd ordered the drinks, he ushered them all to a small table, away from the rest of the crowd, half hidden by an enormous stand of flowers.

"You knew I wasn't regular military straight off, didn't you, Seamus?" he asked as they sat down in the closeted spot.

Seamus shook his head. "Men like you don't like taking orders like ordinary soldiers. No way you changed that much in the three years since I last saw you."

"You might be right about that. The fact is…" He paused as the bartender arrived with the drinks, set them down, and left. "The fact is, I wanted to speak to you and Michael. With your wives' permission, of course."

"Both of us?" Seamus looked bewildered.

He nodded. "I'm part of a new organization tasked with collecting the most valuable thing in this war—information. This is a new kind of conflict. Battles will be won before they're ever fought by the side that knows what the other one is thinking."

"Why are you telling us this?" Michael asked.

"Have you enlisted yet, young man?"

"I'm signing up tomorrow. I'm thinking about becoming a flyer in the Army Air Forces."

"A noble ambition, but let me tell you who we're recruiting."

"Who's 'we?'" Lisa asked sharply.

"I'm a member of a new organization called the Office of Strategic Services. We're so new that we don't officially exist yet, but that'll happen in the next few months. We're recruiting a special type of person to help with the war effort: people who can live a double life, people who can walk through the world without giving anything away, people with impeccable German accents."

Michael shook his head regretfully. "I only spent four years in Germany, so I don't speak like a native. And I'm not nearly devious enough for your organization, Mr. Hayden. I believe anything anyone tells me, and I know from my wife that my face is an open book. Besides, my heart is set on flying."

Hayden smiled with gentle regret. "I'm sorry to hear deviousness doesn't run in the family. Your father and I had a valuable relationship in Berlin."

"You did?" Michael looked sharply at Seamus, who blushed and glanced at Hayden.

"Tell him," grinned the so-called 'colonel'.

"Are you sure?" He took a deep breath. "Okay... Michael, Lisa, Monika. This man Hayden was my handler in Berlin when I worked as an asset for the US State Department..."

Monika felt excitement stirring within her as she listened to her father-in-law's story. She wondered if Seamus Ritter still had some information to provide about his old contacts in Berlin.

"But I don't think there's much I can do to help you either,

Bill," Seamus said disappointingly. "All my old contacts are gone. I know nothing of value now."

"Another shame. We need recruits who thrive on danger and excitement, who have an appetite for the unconventional, like yourself, Ritter."

"I'm not sure I ever did thrive on danger, Hayden. I was just a conventional, ordinary man trying to do his duty. I'd recommend my daughter Maureen, but she's in the South of France right now, and she has her hands full with the Jewish children she's hiding. I don't know when she'll be back in America."

"A pity."

"So, it's not just men you're recruiting?" Monika asked in surprise.

The tall man smiled at her. "Not at all. We're not bound by convention. We're very interested in women too. We want someone equally honest and devious, inconspicuous and audacious, quick and prudent, zealous and cool. I want a cat burglar with morals. I don't care if that person's a woman or a man. In fact, women have proven very successful behind the lines in France."

Her heart was on fire. "You're actively recruiting?"

He looked at her more closely, his smile fading. "Every day. We're going to need the bravest and the best."

"Then take me."

Michael nearly dropped his beer in horror. "What are you talking about, Monika?"

"Monika, please..." Lisa was clearly shocked.

'Your place is here with us, Monika," said her father-in-law gently but firmly.

"No, it's not." She was so excited she could hardly breathe. It was as if someone had offered her a chance to fly. "No one will let me work for the war effort here because they know I'm German. But that's my greatest asset in work like this. I know Berlin and the surrounding area like I designed the place myself. I survived alone in the city for two years after my father was taken away."

"Your father was arrested?" Hayden seemed fascinated.

She kept her face expressionless as she answered. She would show him how icy cold she could be, how unreadable. "He died in a concentration camp in '36. He was a trade union leader. The official letter said he had slipped in the shower. They never sent the body."

"And you were on your own? No mother or siblings?"

"It was just me. My mother died when I was 12. I had to learn how to survive on my own after my father was taken."

"And what age were you then?"

"I was 16."

"What is this, Monika?" Michael protested. "You have a life here. There's plenty you can do to help the war effort in America. Isn't that true, Mr. Hayden?"

But Hayden didn't seem to even hear her husband. He was staring into Monika's eyes. He reached into his pocket and pulled out a business card. "I have to leave tomorrow morning. I'll be back at the office in DC for the rest of the week. Think about our conversation and give me a call."

Monika took the card and held it in her palm. It felt almost hot, burning.

Hayden rose to his feet. "I'd better go and work the room a little more. Plenty of seven-figure types in here with guilty consciences. Enjoy, all of you. Drink as much champagne or beer as you wish. It's all on us. It was great to see you again, Seamus. Maybe we will work together someday. Goodbye, Lisa, Michael, Monika."

"Goodbye, Bill…" Seamus stared in bewilderment after his old friend as he walked away.

Michael was also staring after him, sitting with his hands resting flat on the table, looking very pale.

"Shall we dance?" Lisa asked Seamus, with a quick glance at Monika, who was re-reading the little card.

"Of course. This is my favorite song," he replied obediently, getting to his feet.

As soon as they were out of earshot, Michael turned to her. "What was that about? Don't you think we should talk about things like this first?"

"Isn't that what we're doing now?" she pushed back. "Like we talked about you signing up this morning?"

He pushed a hand through his floppy hair. "We barely got out of Germany alive back in '36. You know what the Nazis are like better than most."

"And that's exactly why I don't intend to sit out the war in New York, without anything useful to do."

"You seriously want to get mixed up with a fake colonel who's touting around some organization that hasn't even formed yet?"

"You were free to choose to serve. Why can't I? Once you leave, there's nothing here for me."

"You have your friends, and my family considers you one of us, you know that. Lisa relies on you."

"She has her daughter and a husband. And this isn't about me being bored. I think about my father every day. I've tried to suppress the anger I feel inside of me over his death, but I can't. I want to avenge him."

"By dying yourself?" The anguish was plain to see in his eyes.

"Who says I'm going to die? This is just a business card in my hand," she tried to reassure him, to take away that look. "Who knows what this will amount to? They might only need me to translate or file papers in German, but I have to make the call at least. I can't just pretend this meeting never happened or that the feelings inside me don't exist. I can't live that life."

Michael glanced towards Lisa on the dance floor. She and Seamus were dancing cheek to cheek.

"My stepmother is German. She suffered at the hands of the Nazis too. Do you think she would make the call to Hayden?"

"I don't know. Everyone has their own life to lead. She has hers, and I have mine. I have to shape mine so I can look myself in the eye when I'm standing in front of the mirror. I don't know what I'm looking for, and I certainly don't know what calling Bill Hayden will lead to, but I'm sure that I have to do it."

Michael took her hands in his. He had tears in his eyes. "I don't think it's a good idea, Monika. I don't know where all of this is going to lead. If anything happened to you—"

"And what about you? I can't bear the thought of you up there with flak bursting all around you." She pushed him away. Tears threatened, but as always, she suppressed them. This wasn't a good time to demonstrate weakness. There was never a good time. "I might be in an office translating papers or filing, and you talk to me about danger?"

"I have to go, Monika. This is something I have to do—for myself and my country."

"Then we feel exactly the same way," she answered.

"But..."

She took his face between her hands and kissed him, cutting off his protests, lingering with her lips against his as if it would be the last time they ever kissed.

"Now, take me back to the dance floor," she said as she drew back. "Let's enjoy this night. Let's enjoy our happiness."

With a somber face, he stood and took her by the hand. As they circled the floor in each other's arms, Monika let all thoughts of the war drift away like dead leaves adrift on the river of her mind.

Nothing was going to come between her and Michael for the rest of this wondrous night.

3

A few days later, Michael was accepted into the new Army Air Forces. After telling Monika, he invited all the family out to lunch at an Italian place downtown to break the news: his father and stepmother, his brother Conor, his sister Fiona, and his little stepsister, Hannah, who was in eighth grade. Only Maureen was absent, still helping the Jewish children in France.

He tried to contain himself until they'd finished eating, but the plates were still on the red-checked tablecloth when he blurted out that he was being shipped off to begin training the following Monday. No one answered for a few seconds. But it was clear that no one was surprised.

Only 22-year-old Fiona, who was working as a secretary in a law firm, spoke up. "Do you have any idea what you're getting into, Michael? Pilots get shot down all the time."

"Someone has to do it."

"And I'm next," said his younger brother, Conor, eagerly. "I'm joining up as soon as I hit 18 in November. I'm not going to be the only guy I know too yellow to pick up a rifle. No one's going to tell me I can't." He looked pointedly at his father, as if expecting to be questioned.

"Dad?" Fiona also looked at her father.

Seamus Ritter cleared his throat and passed his hand over his eyes. "I'm proud of you both," he said. "Of all of you."

His wife, Lisa, slipped one arm around him and the other around her daughter, Hannah. "This could be the last time we're all together for a while," she said quietly to the assembled family. "This war's going to get a lot worse before it gets better. We know more than most in this country how strong the Nazis are."

"That's why I have to do my part," Michael said, glancing at Monika.

"And mine," Conor added fiercely.

Fiona didn't speak. No one ever talked of her time with the League of German Girls, the female Hitler Youth in the 30s. She clammed up most times anyone mentioned Hitler these days, though she and her troop had performed for him before the Olympic Games in Berlin back in '36. She raised a finger to a passing waitress and ordered a bottle of wine for the table.

"Then we should enjoy our time together while we still can," she said.

"Hear, hear," her father said, smiling gratefully at her. "I just wish Maureen was here with us... "

"Her and the gorgeous Christophe," Fiona said. "I can't wait to meet him."

"Nor me. I think he sounds very charming," Hannah said cheekily.

Her mother laughed and frowned, shaking her head. "You're too young to be thinking about boys, Hannah."

"Maureen's safe, for now, anyway," said Seamus. "The Germans haven't made it to Marseilles yet. The refugees in the safe houses in Izieu are doing well. She's still working on getting them out."

"She's not doing anything too dangerous, I hope?" Monika asked.

"You know Maureen," her father said with less confidence than Monika expected. "Anything's possible with that girl. Life over there is hard. The rationing and shortages are beginning to bite, but she seemed content in her last letter, and Christophe is looking after her."

"I'm sure it's more like she's looking after him," Fiona laughed.

The wine arrived, and once everyone had a glass in front of them, Monika felt emboldened to speak. "I'm hoping to do my bit for the war effort too."

Fiona nodded. "As a nurse, or something? Or I might be able to get you a job in my office?"

"No actually, I'm hoping to put my German to use."

"Really?" asked Michael in a harsher tone than she'd expected. "I thought we'd decided against this."

"You might have," she said equally sharply. "But I haven't."

An awkward silence descended on the table, and then Michael started talking about the ball game to his father as if the conversation was over. But Monika wasn't about to lie down. In the days following the party at the Plaza Hotel, she had called Hayden, and she and Michael had discussed his subsequent offer several times. The offer was vague and open-ended. But whatever it was, she wanted it. Michael, sensing a terrible danger, was against it. Now, he seemed to think the fact that she hadn't mentioned it for a whole day meant she'd given up on the idea.

Conor was looking curiously from one of them to the other. "What are you talking about, Monika?"

"I met an old friend of your father at a war bonds event in the Plaza last weekend. He's setting up a new group, and he seemed interested in me and what I might have to offer." She spoke firmly while Michael sat back with his arms folded, his lips pressed tightly together.

"And what do they want you for?" asked Fiona seriously.

"I'm not completely sure. I expect I'm going to help with translations." Saying that much out loud seemed safe enough. She wasn't sure if she should be talking about Hayden and his new organization at all. They'd all seen the newsreels stating how "loose lips sink ships."

Lisa smiled encouragingly at her. "Well, that sounds safe enough, and perfect for your skill set. When do you begin training?"

"I don't know yet. He says he'll call when they're up and running and find work for me."

"You'd be a credit to any organization you joined," Seamus said. He also seemed relieved his old friend was only offering his daughter-in-law a humble desk job. "Wouldn't she, Michael?"

"Yes," Monika's husband answered slowly. "They'd be lucky to have her."

Monika smiled at him for not betraying her. She knew he suspected there might be a lot more to this than a desk job. "Thank you, Michael," she said.

He looked at her, pain in his eyes. "Is this really what you want?"

"More than anything."

He put his hand on hers. "You never were one to back down."

It was the nearest he'd got so far to giving her permission. Not that she needed it. Michael was her husband, not her master. While it meant a lot, his approval was far from the deciding factor as to whether she'd go forward. She had no intention of sitting out the war in a foreign city while her home country went up in flames, particularly with her husband gone. The truth was she'd made the decision as soon as Hayden told her about his new venture. It was up to her to decide what her life would be.

Seamus raised his glass. "To all my brave children, here and in France. May you remain safe in the service of our country and our way of life. We all saw what Hitler did to Germany. Every person around this table has experienced the evils and horror of Nazism in one way or the other. Who better than the Ritters to stop it?"

They all clinked their glasses and settled back in their seats. Once they'd finished that bottle of wine, Seamus ordered another, and lunch turned into an early dinner. They reveled in each other's company. Monika looked around the table at the only family she'd known these past six years, but her love for them wasn't going to hold her back. Nothing would.

For what seemed like the hundredth time, Monika picked up the phone in the apartment where she now lived alone and dialed the number for Bill Hayden's office in Washington, DC. She held the card in her hand as she made the call, even though she had no need to look at it. The number was ingrained in her mind, and she was sure she'd remember it for the rest of her life.

As always, the phone rang a few times before the secretary picked it up.

"Hello, Gladys," Monika said. "Guess who?"

"Hello, Miss Ritter."

"Is Mr. Hayden available? Please say yes. My birthday is coming up."

"I'm sorry, Miss Ritter, Mr. Hayden is out of the office today."

"Is he ever in? You told me to call back today."

"His plans changed at the last minute."

"When is he going to be available? I last spoke to him five months ago. He said he'd call when he needed me. When is he going to let me know?"

"As I told you before—"

"I know he was away for most of the summer. But he's back in the office now, isn't he?"

"From time to time."

"Gladys, do you get the impression that I'm not going to stop calling until I speak to Mr. Hayden?"

The secretary laughed out loud but then stopped herself and said, "To the best of my knowledge, he'll be in the office tomorrow."

"Gladys, have you ever wondered what I look like?"

"On occasion." She could hear the laughter bubbling up again.

"Well, you'll find out tomorrow when I come down there. Tell Mr. Hayden he can expect me first thing in the morning."

She hung up the phone. The apartment was quiet. The only sound was of the traffic on the street outside.

She walked into the bedroom she'd shared with Michael. His clothes were still in the closet, and the latest letter he'd sent from Air Force training was on the nightstand. The nights before she fell asleep were when she felt his absence the most, and again in the morning when she woke in an empty bed.

Now she sat on that empty bed, her heart aching for him as she picked up his letter to reread it.

It was hot in Georgia. After completing his 65 hours of flight training at the primary level a few weeks before, Michael was about to move on to his basic flight training when he'd begin to fly solo and specialize in the type of plane he'd one day fly over enemy territory. It was a short letter, just one page. He promised to write again soon and ended with the assertion that he was counting down the days to when he'd see her again— just after training ended before he shipped out to England.

Monika put down the letter and, after giving herself a quiet moment to worry about her husband, she walked over to the closet and packed some clothes into a suitcase.

She left the apartment a few minutes later and took a cab to the bus station. She sat at the front of the bus, relieved to be beside an old woman—at least she wouldn't have to spend the journey fending off the unwanted attention of young men. Things had changed since the war began. She'd been used to men staring at her entire adult life. It started when she was about 12 when Oliver Strauss expressed his love for her in a letter after her mother died. But lately, the number of suitors approaching her had spiraled out of control. People said it was because of the war. With the threat of imminent death hanging over them, the young men felt they had little to lose despite the sight of her wedding ring. Usually, a few curt words in her German accent was enough to fend them off, though it had also led to several ugly incidents.

Monika was outside Hayden's office before nine o'clock the next morning. She hadn't been sure how to dress at first, but ultimately, she'd opted for a pretty navy dress she loved. She'd spent ten minutes on her makeup. Hayden was a man, after all, and she intended to use every weapon at her disposal to get what she needed.

The street, in an area of the city called Foggy Bottom, looked like any other, and the sign on the doorway offered no clue as to what was inside. A convenient bench at the corner five yards away provided her a place to watch the door from, and the newspaper she bought offered the perfect cover.

She became absorbed in a story about a ship called The Laconia that had been torpedoed by the Germans off the coast of Africa, with the loss of almost 1,700 lives—most of them

Italian prisoners-of-war being transported away from the battlefields in Europe. Monika found herself amazed at how such incidents were treated with little shock in wartime. Before the outbreak of war, an incident like this would have been massive news. More people died on the Laconia than the Titanic, but in a war where things like this happened every day, it was relegated below the fold on the front page.

Then, just after 9:30, she heard a car door slam and looked up. Bill Hayden had just gotten out of a car and was strolling toward the office door. Suppressing a wave of irritation that he could look so casual, she jumped up and hurried down the street. "Mr. Hayden! It's Monika Ritter."

Hayden stopped and turned, and a look of surprised recognition came over his face. "Well, kid, there ought to be a picture of you in the dictionary beside the definition for persistence. How many times have you called me now?"

"I haven't been counting, have you?" she asked pertly.

He laughed and shook his head. "You want to come inside?"

"That's why I came all the way here on the bus."

"I have a meeting with someone in a few minutes. Maybe I'll introduce you to them, since you've come all this way. Persistence and initiative are qualities we need."

Monika nodded. It didn't seem right to appear gleeful in front of someone who'd been dodging her attention for so long, but inside, she was elated. He opened the door with a key from his pocket and led her up a flight of stairs to an office that read "Dalton Painting" in black writing on the translucent glass. She assumed the pretty blonde woman in her 30s, who was sitting behind the desk, was Gladys. She winked at Monika as she walked in behind her boss.

"Mrs. Ritter, I presume," she said.

"Gladys. I feel like I know you. And may I say you're even lovelier than you sound on the phone."

"Ah, Gladys!" Hayden looked mockingly reproachful. "Are

you telling me you knew this young lady was about to pounce and didn't warn me?"

The secretary answered with a smile and a shake of her head. "Only since yesterday, sir, and I had no way of contacting you. Besides, I thought she deserved her chance after all this time."

"Any other visitors you'd care to mention?"

"Mr. Dulles is already waiting in your office."

"Perfect. Come inside with me, Monika."

Hayden opened the door to his office and held it for Monika as she walked through. A slim man in a pinstriped suit with thinning gray hair and a matching mustache stood up to greet them.

"Good morning, Bill," he said.

"Good morning, Allen. I've brought someone to meet you." He put his hand on Monika's shoulder, pushing her forward a few inches. "This is the young woman I've kept telling you about, who's called me every other day for the last five months. I found her outside on the sidewalk waiting for me when I arrived this morning. Monika Ritter, Allen Dulles."

"What a pleasure to meet you at last." The man shook Monika's hand.

"Likewise." She had a burning desire to ask why they hadn't called her back if they were so interested in her but decided this wasn't the time.

"As I've told you, Allen, Monika's from Berlin. She hustled there to stay alive when she was a girl," Hayden said. "I worked with her now father-in-law when I was over there. He's a good man, and I like his son as well. Very honest and open. I think this girl could be someone we can trust."

Dulles drew a pipe from his pocket and began to fill it with tobacco. "I spent a little time in Berlin myself about eight or nine years ago, Monika. You know the city well?"

"I could draw a map of the place blindfolded, sir."

"Why don't you sit down?" he asked, pointing to a chair facing the desk. "How long have you been in the States, Monika?"

"I left Germany after the games in '36. I had to escape with the man whom I went on to marry and his sister after we had some trouble with the police. I was in Paris until '39 when we came to America. My husband's in the Army Air Force now. I want to do my bit."

Dulles then asked a few questions about how and when she'd been left as an orphan. "Why didn't you go to your uncle and aunt in Ulm when your father was taken away?"

"After Hitler came to power, my uncle worked his way up the ladder. The last I heard, he was one of the regional heads of the Gestapo in Baden-Württemberg, but that was before I left."

"What's this man's name?" Dulles asked.

"Dieter Berben."

He tamped down his pipe. "I'll be sure to look him up. When did you last have contact with him?"

"The last time we visited was in the summer of '33. He and my father had a row over the Nazis, and we never returned. He and my aunt sent a card when my dad died, but nothing more. I'm sure you see now why I didn't go stay with them."

"Did they ever suspect you of being disloyal to Hitler?"

"Indirectly, perhaps. I don't know. I haven't thought about Uncle Dieter in years."

"What did you do to survive on your own?" Dulles asked as gray smoke filled the air around him.

"I danced with rich men at the Hotel Adlon in Berlin."

"I know the place," Dulles said, glancing at Hayden, who had sat down behind the desk. "You got to know these men?"

"Yes. And I had a plan. It sounds a little crazy now, but I heard about Goebbels' penchant for pretty girls. My idea was to get close enough to slit his throat. I knew I'd never get close enough to Hitler."

"No. He has no interest in women. All he cares about is the cause." The slim man sat back and puffed on his pipe for a few seconds. He seemed to be taking it all in, considering what to do.

Monika hoped she hadn't ruined her chances by admitting to such recklessness. She dipped into her bag for her cigarettes, hoping they wouldn't spot the slight tremble of her hand.

Hayden reached into his desk drawer for an ashtray and pushed it across the table for both her and Dulles to use.

"So...What is it you want to do, Mrs. Ritter?" Dulles asked, blowing out a ring of smoke.

Her heart leaped with hope. "Whatever you need me to do, Mr. Dulles, that's why I'm here. That's why I've been trying to join since I met Mr. Hayden in New York in April."

Hayden smiled at her across the desk, his eyebrows raised. "And I think you've proved yourself with your tenacity. Allen, why don't you tell her where things stand, and we'll see if she's interested."

Allen Dulles nodded and leaned forward. "Right then. Now, Monika, I joined the OSS last year. And I'm currently in the process of putting together a team. I've been in negotiations with the Swiss government. They've agreed to let us set up an operation in Bern. From there, we'll be able to monitor the situation in France, Austria, and even Germany."

"Have any agents been sent into Germany yet?" Monika asked.

Hayden laughed. "Steady! That's classified information."

"Would that be something you'd be interested in doing?" Dulles asked, intrigued.

"I have unfinished business there," she responded.

"Returning to the Reich, eh?" The spymaster said with a smile. "We're recruiting women as well as men. What we've seen in France and the other occupied countries is that they can move more freely and blend into the crowd without raising suspicion."

"I'm very interested," she said. "I'll go tomorrow."

"You haven't trained yet," Hayden said, amused.

"When can you begin training?" Dulles asked, more seriously.

"I have some clothes in a suitcase at the hotel I'm staying in. I don't need to go back to New York."

"That's the spirit!" Dulles turned to his colleague. "Can you get her out to one of the parks?"

"I can arrange for her to be brought to Catoctin tomorrow morning if she agrees," Hayden said. "Is that what you want, Mrs. Ritter?" asked Dulles.

"I don't know. What is Catoctin?"

"We have appropriated some of our national parks for training," Hayden said. "Catoctin is a forest in Maryland a few miles northwest of here. A truck's leaving the city tomorrow with recruits for training. I could put you on it if you like, though it means you'd end up in Bern rather than Berlin. Would you like to think about it? Do you have people you need to say goodbye to?"

Monika thought of her husband's family in New York. She could call them tonight. They didn't need any more of a goodbye than that. She had to do this, and the appointment in Switzerland would be a good start. She felt she couldn't afford to delay her answer. Dulles and Hayden were looking for decisive, independent people.

"Put me on that truck."

"Where are you staying in Washington? I'll be in touch as soon as I know what's what."

"That's what you said in New York," Monika responded with a wry smile as she wrote down her address.

He grinned at her. "I wasn't sure you wanted it then. Now I know you do."

"You didn't get that impression from all the phone calls and letters?"

He laughed. "I did, and I was going to call you next week and invite you down to see me."

"She's got spirit, this one," Dulles said.

"Does she ever!"

"I'll be waiting," Monika said and walked out.

She said goodbye to Gladys and descended to the street. It was a fine morning in the city. She looked around and then up at the sky. The faint outline of a plane was visible against the powder blue sky behind it. She thought of her husband and what he'd say but walked on as she realized that it didn't matter now. The die was cast.

4
―――

Michael felt beads of sweat trickling down his forehead as the driver announced their imminent arrival at Douglas Airfield. The olive-drab uniform he wore was wet at the armpits, and the smell of body odor hung heavily in the enclosed space. The cadets at the windows peered out as the bus pulled up. There was a runway and five large hangars to his left containing planes he recognized as PT-17s, single-engine training planes that the German or Japanese fighters would tear to shreds. He had already flown some in primary training, with an instructor in the back barking orders at him and criticizing his every move as if their lives depended on it. It seemed the instructors' job, as much as imparting the skills needed to fly, was to weed out the weakest recruits—those who might crack under the pressure of flak exploding around them in the air or the impending threat of Messerschmidt 109s screaming at them from below.

That was why almost half the class had already dropped out, or "washed out," as the Air Force phrase went. The ones that were left came from several different training airfields, and he didn't know most of them.

As the driver got up to open the doors, Ronald Lawson, a recruit Michael had bunked with since they began primary training nine weeks before, nudged him in the ribs with a smile. "I guess we're in the big boys' school now," he said in his Texan drawl. "No more three hours lectures to put us to sleep. We're going flying all the time!" Lawson was from Dallas, the youngest of four brothers, all in the Army Air Force. He was 24 and had been married since he was 17. He took a photo of his wife and three young children out of his wallet and kissed it before he stood up. Michael filed off the bus after him, and they stood to attention with the other recruits on the tarmac. An officer came to greet them. He was slight, with a tanned, handsome face, and didn't look much older than 25.

"Welcome to Douglas Airfield. For those who don't know, we're in Georgia, gentlemen." Several recruits laughed, and he smiled slightly before he continued. "This is the beginning of basic training. Each man here has already completed their 65 hours of flying time during primary training but let me assure you that was a cakewalk compared to what you're about to face. My name is Captain Hart, and you might find me tough, but how I and the other instructors treat you is nothing in comparison to the reception you'll get when you're flying over Germany in a few months' time. Our job is to prepare you for every eventuality so you don't have to think when you're under fire. Everything can change in a second up there."

He pointed up at the sky, and Michael followed his eyes. Above, the blue sky was wreathed in clouds.

"The second you take to react could mean the difference between life and death for you and your crew up there," said the captain. 'And you are not allowed to die. That is the first rule. You may have seen death already. What we're doing here is a dangerous pursuit. I am sick of caskets of burned-up recruits leaving this airfield. If you are not focused, if you are dreaming about your little sweetheart waiting for you back in

Biloxi or Brooklyn and whether she's making eyes at the milkman, you will hesitate, and let me assure you, gentlemen, that's a surefire way to guarantee a trip back home—in a body bag!" Hart's face contorted in what Michael could have sworn was a look of pain. "Notice the scorch marks on the runway just over there."

The black blotches on the asphalt were a few yards from where they were standing. Michael wondered about the man or men who'd died there.

"If you're not ready to focus, or commit totally to being here, step forward now. There's no shame in being a bombardier or a glider pilot. We need those." No one moved. "But if you're prepared to be the best, to put aside the life you know beyond this place and follow what your instructors tell you as if they were the words of our Lord and Savior Jesus Christ himself for the next nine weeks, come with me. This is a big step up from what you've previously known. Welcome to the 63rd Flying Training Detachment."

Several of the men cheered as they followed him across the tarmac. Captain Hart walked at the same pace that most people ran, and they covered the ground between the bus and the modern, newly built barracks in no time at all.

"Find your bunks!" Hart shouted as he led them inside.

The interior of the barracks was clean and freshly painted. The beds were made to perfection.

"This ain't bad at all," Lawson said. "I could make this home for a few weeks. Flip a coin for top?" Michael nodded as his friend took a nickel out of his pocket.

"Heads."

Lawson tossed the coin. "Looks like you're out of luck, Michael," he said as he revealed tails.

Michael threw his pack on the bottom bunk.

"All right," Hart yelled. "Join me outside in thirty seconds. Move it, gentlemen, this isn't a country club."

Moments later, the recruits were lined up outside again, where Hart was waiting to bring them over to the mess hall.

Michael was relieved it was time for the midday meal; he was starving. And the food was good—better than in primary training. Michael had the feeling that the men here had already proven themselves enough to merit better treatment.

"Good chow," Fred Sackler, a cadet from Detroit, said.

"Don't they say the condemned men get the best food just before the execution?" Lawson said. "Though I thought they'd give even better to the big Olympic star over here beside me."

Michael winced and didn't look up.

"I knew I recognized you from somewhere, Ritter," a man whose name badge read Tate said. "You were in the 100-metre finals in the Olympics back in '36. Running for Germany."

"Thanks, Lawson," Michael said, shooting his friend a dark look.

"I gotta let the guys know who they'll be flying with. Sure, it's not your fault you had to run for the wrong team."

"I remember you now," Sackler eagerly added. "You were the guy who lost to Jesse Owens."

"Just what I always wanted to be remembered for," Michael said. "That doesn't narrow it down, though, does it? Everyone lost to Owens."

"No, but you're the guy," Tate said. "I read about you in the papers. You're the one who got injured in the final but still didn't stop."

"Yeah, the most famous loser at the games," Michael said grimly.

"No way, man," Lawson said. "You were cheered out of that stadium. Even your opponents were on their feet."

Michael cast his mind back to the Olympiastadion in Berlin and what had been the culmination of years of training. He couldn't think back to that time and not think of Monika. That was when he met the beautiful, mysterious girl who became his wife.

"So, what are you doing in the American Air Force?" asked Sackler.

"There's no Olympics because of the war. And I wanted to do my bit just like you boys."

One of the younger cadets, a man from Tennessee called Griffin, whom he vaguely knew from having met in the queue for the bus, leaned forward to speak. "You still that fast?"

"Not as much as when I was running in the games, but I'm probably quicker than most."

"I sprinted in high school. My coach seemed to think I had what it took to make it to the games. You look all washed up to me!"

Lawson banged the table with both hands. "Oh, I feel a bet coming on, boys! I can smell it!"

"You wanna see if you can beat me?" Griffin grinned.

Michael was used to these kinds of challenges. He pretended to stifle a yawn. "Are you sure? I don't want to show you up in front of the other guys."

The men at the table hollered with excitement, but Michael wasn't being entirely facetious. He didn't want to humiliate the young man, even if he was shooting his mouth off.

Lawson assumed the role of organizer. "All right. Let's figure this out. How about we set up a track on the runway after dinner tonight?"

"A hundred meters, and give him a five-meter start," Michael said casually.

"I don't need no five-meter start, old man," Griffin protested, stung.

The men reacted with more hoots and hollers.

"Five bucks says I can beat you with a five-yard start," Michael answered.

"We got a deal."

"Done."

Lawson took his opportunity to grasp the limelight. "All right, gentlemen, get your bets in. With the five-meter start for the kid, it'll be 2-1 for Griffin."

Several men thrust their money forward, about half going for each man. Michael shook his head again. Lawson winked at him as he accepted another wad of cash from one of the other cadets.

Hart was waiting with three other instructors outside when the men emerged from the mess hall. They brought the cadets to the first of the five hangars beside the runway. Several single-engine planes were taxiing out onto the runway from other hangars. Michael stood and watched one take off. Even after all the time he'd already spent in the air, the principle of flight still seemed like a miracle to him. But, wary of being seen not paying attention, he made sure to face Hart as soon as the captain began to speak.

"This is the AT-10 Wichita." Hart gestured up at the silver twin-engine plane sitting behind him in a row of half a dozen. "You are standing here with me today because you have indicated a preference to fly bombers when you graduate."

"If you graduate," one of the other instructors said.

"And believe me, that "if" is one of the biggest words you'll ever encounter," Hart said, looking hard at them all before continuing. "The AT-10 was designed specifically to train cadets like yourselves. I know you're all dying to get into the cockpit of a B25 or even a Flying Fortress, but you're not ready to handle a fickle mistress like a heavy bomber yet. Think of the AT-10 as your high school girlfriend, preparing you so you don't disappoint your wife on your wedding night later on." A few of the men sniggered as Hart pressed on. "We'll begin training in these magnificent machines tomorrow, and you'll be expected to log 25 hours of landings with an instructor before you take it solo. All in good time. But for now, you're going to have to content yourselves with some PT."

The cadets groaned before returning to the barracks to change for the five-mile run they were about to embark on.

After a grueling day of physical training, they returned to the mess hall for dinner. The last thing Michael felt like doing was racing Griffin, but it seemed the younger man had counted on as much.

"You're not gonna chicken out on our race, are you?" he grinned as they sat down.

"Not a chance."

"My boy here is ready," Lawson said, wrapping his hand around Michael's neck. He waited until Griffin walked away to whisper in Michael's ear, " Are you really ready for this?"

"I don't think I'll beat my personal best, but he just went through the same thing I did."

"Yes, he did. That's the spirit."

Word must have gotten back to the powers that be, but rather than stop the race, they seemed to approve of the competition and had placed their own bets. When Michael arrived in his training outfit, and the shoes he'd been running in before dinner, Captain Hart and several other instructors were already waiting with at least 50 men,

Lawson and some others had just finished measuring out 100 meters exactly, just like in the Olympics; they'd put down cones to mark the lanes. "You ready for the race, gentlemen?" Lawson said to the officers.

Hart gave a thumbs up. "Lead on!"

Michael limbered up as he walked to the farthest cone, five yards behind Griffin, who was also in his training outfit and looked very slender and fit.

Lawson came over to Michael, looking a bit anxious now,

having taken so many bets. If Michael lost, he'd be broke. "How're you feeling, champ? You sure about this head start?"

Michael shrugged. "I don't usually run after an afternoon of PT, and my dinner is feeling pretty heavy in my stomach right now, but I guess I'll be all right."

"That's the spirit," his friend said, looking even more worried.

Griffin yelled over his shoulder, "I'm looking forward to showing up that washed-up-has-been!"

Lawson rolled his eyes at Michael. "You hear that?"

"Everyone heard that," Michael replied, as Lawson laughed nervously.

Blocking Griffin out of his head, Michael continued his warm-up routine. He removed his mind from the situation, imagining himself with Monika by a cool mountain stream. He drew in several deep breaths.

Tate had a pistol and ordered the runners to the starting line. With no blocks, each man crouched down on their hands with one knee on the ground. Griffin glanced back over his shoulder at Michael and winked at him. Michael didn't react. He'd seen it all before. This kid thought he was something special. Perhaps he was. Michael wasn't going to underestimate him. He stared down the runway at the finishing line 100 meters away. Hart and another officer were stationed there to declare the winner in case it was close. Michael had no intention of needing them.

The starter called out, and the men raised their heels. Griffin went before the gun, but no one called it, and Michael found himself six meters behind instead of five. The crowd on the sidelines had swelled to over a hundred, and the cadets whooped and hollered as the men sprinted.

The kid was fast, but he was too upright. A stiff breeze sprung up in front of them, and Michael closed on Griffin as the wind slowed the younger man down. The finish line was fast approaching, but Michael was closing in with every stride. He hurtled forward, ducking down to finish ahead of Griffin, but the younger man ran straight on with his arms raised. He was quick, and Michael had only just pipped him by a nose.

Griffin didn't seem to care about what had actually happened and jumped in the air, celebrating a victory he didn't earn. Men who'd bet on him surrounded him, perhaps thinking if they celebrated too, Lawson would pay up. Michael laughed and sauntered back to Captain Hart and the other instructor, a tall man called Haglund.

"Are you going to tell the kid he lost or am I?" he asked them.

"I don't know," Haglund said. "It was close."

"No way," Lawson said. "Michael beat him, and besides, Griffin jumped the gun at the start."

Griffin came running over. "You're not going to try to steal that race, are you? I won it, fair and square."

Lawson didn't entertain his lies. "You jumped the gun, Griffin, and you still lost!"

Several men around them agreed with Lawson, but the cadets who'd backed Griffin weren't backing down.

"What do you think, Hart? Your call," said Haglund laconically. "I've no idea one way or the other, and I had a bet on Griffin, so I don't think I should have the last word."

"I had money on Griffin as well," Hart admitted. "I've seen him run before, and he had a five-meter start, which is immense. I wasn't at the starting line, so I don't know about him jumping the gun, but I was right here at the end. I saw Ritter bend down at the line and come through. Ritter won it."

Relieved on Lawson's behalf, Michael smiled and held out his hand to his opponent. "Good race, Griffin. Your coach was right."

The young hothead didn't shake his hand and stormed off, muttering about Michael having run as a German in the

Olympics. A crowd of argumentative cadets surrounded Lawson, trying to recoup their winnings, still protesting that the younger man had won or that it was too tight to call. Michael walked away with the instructors, not envious of the predicament his friend had put himself in but confident of the Texan's ability to win the day and still remain friends with everyone who'd lost their money to him.

After a day of getting to know the controls, the time came to fly the new aircraft. Michael had never flown a twin-engine plane before and felt a bristle of nerves as he walked toward the hangar. Still giddy about the considerable sum of money he'd made on the race, Lawson didn't seem to be experiencing any such trepidation. He hooted and hollered as he strolled out. "Woo-eh! I've been waiting for this," he said. "The first dress rehearsal for our introduction to Adolf!"

"There's no bombs on these planes and no Nazis to drop 'em on in Georgia, either," Michael said with a chuckle. He felt his nerves easing. That was one of the reasons he liked Lawson so much—the calming effect he had on everyone around him.

"But this is the next step, ain't it?" Lawson said. "Next thing you know, we'll be shoving a five hundred-pounder up Hitler's behind!"

"Come on, Lawson," snapped an instructor called Jansen, who was waiting to bring the big Texan up.

"Good luck!" Michael called after Lawson.

"You don't need luck when you're as good as I am, Ritter," the Texan hollered with a big wave.

"Ritter, you're with me," barked a different instructor, whose name Michael didn't know, "Follow me and do everything I say." He brought Michael over to the nearest AT-10, and Michael climbed into the two-man cockpit.

"I'm Captain Thomas," the man said, getting in behind him. "Familiarize yourself with the controls before we taxi out."

Michael located the compass before moving his eyes to the fuel level, the engine temperature gauge, and the landing gear. He put his hands on the yoke and his feet on the rudder pedals.

"Start the engine when you're ready," Thomas said.

Michael did as he was told and let out the throttle. He was cautious as he taxied out onto the runway. Lawson was already in the air with Captain Jansen. Michael wasn't surprised but wasn't about to rush this just because his friend had. He spared a quick thought for Monika as he always did in these moments but then pushed her from his mind. These moments were too dangerous not to be fully focused on the task at hand.

"It's your turn," the instructor said beside him. "Move into position and get us in the air."

The blue sky on the horizon beckoned, and the familiar giddy excitement Michael always felt at these moments washed through him. It was similar to what he used to feel running the 100 meters. His mind harkened back to the '36 Olympics and the call of the crowd as he'd lined up on the starting blocks against Jesse Owens. He brought it back as he let out the throttle again, and the plane began to pick up speed.

"She's heavy," he commented as he pulled back on the yoke to bring it into the air.

"Not like the rinky-dink toys you're used to, is it? Level it off at ten thousand feet and watch your speed. She won't go past 200 miles an hour, but don't let her close to that."

The ground dropped behind them as they flew toward the sun in a cloudless sky. The controls were sluggish, and Michael struggled to master them. Thomas barked in his ear, jumping on any tiny mistake he made.

He ordered Michael to make a 90-degree turn and roared at him when it was closer to 85.

"Be exact. No mistakes!" Thomas said.

Michael ensured that the wings were at the correct angle as he tried it again but received no compliment for pulling it off on the second attempt. The one thing every instructor he'd ever flown with had in common was their need to demean and belittle the cadets at every turn. Michael had had no idea how much there was to flying when he enlisted. It was the hardest work he'd ever done, even more so than training for the Olympics. And at least sprinting didn't flirt with the specter of imminent death at every moment.

Michael had fought like the devil every day since he'd joined to keep up, and it was only getting more challenging. But still, even with everything he and the other cadets faced, the freedom of being in the air was like nothing he'd ever experienced. He took a moment to look down at the earth from above when Thomas wasn't looking. The elation of being thousands of feet above the ground had never faded, not since the first time he flew. He smiled to himself as he saw the tiny airfield thousands of feet below and the hills and fields beyond it. The sun had a way of twinkling up here that he'd never seen on the ground, and nothing in the world could ever be quite so blue as the sky above the clouds.

He tried to imagine the terror of flak bursting all around him and of enemy fighters roaring at him hundreds of miles an hour faster than he could ever go with the express intention of killing him and all his friends. No matter how he tried, he knew he'd never fathom the terror of that happening until he was in that moment. It was hard to anticipate a level of fear he'd almost never felt. Preparing his body for that amount of stress was impossible, but the instructors still tried.

"The port engine is failing!" Thomas shouted.

Michael emerged from his trance with a jolt but knew the instructor was lying. He hadn't felt anything. The plane was as steady as the rocky hills on the horizon below. But he knew what Thomas was trying to do. Michael checked the gauges and waited for instructions.

"The engine is on fire. Put it out," the captain ordered.

Michael brought the plane into a dive and waited until Thomas was satisfied that he'd extinguished the imaginary fire before leveling off. Then he climbed to 10,000 feet again, and they cruised for a while before Captain Thomas had him execute some more turns and barrel rolls. Michael saw other planes around them—all of them were other cadets training.

"Bring her home," Thomas said after an hour or so. "We'll wait our turn to land."

Michael circled the airfield as the other cadets landed their planes. The radio tower told him he and Lawson were the last two planes in the sky. Michael looked around for his friend but didn't spot him. Undeterred, he slowed the plane's ascent and lowered the landing gear. The landing went off without a hitch, and Michael turned to his instructor after he'd taxied the plane back into place beside the others. "How was that?"

"Not bad, but try doing that with flak dotting the sky all around you and bullets flying at the cockpit. You still have a lot to learn, Ritter."

Thomas unstrapped himself and got out. Michael tried not to feel disappointed at the instructor's evaluation. These men were not known for their encouraging words. As he climbed down, he heard sirens and turned to see a fire truck speeding toward the runway. Yet there was no accident. Was it a training drill? The men jumped out of the truck, looking up. Michael's blood ran cold as he realized who was flying the only plane left up there.

Then the AT-10 came into his view over the trees, but without the sound that usually accompanied it. An eerie silence followed in the plane's wake.

Thomas had stopped by the runway to watch in horror as

the plane dropped. It was obvious that neither pilot could control her.

"The engines are out!" Michael said, running up beside him.

"They're coming in too fast," Thomas said. "The nose is too low."

Michael could only watch as the plane careered toward the runway.

"Come on, Lawson," he whispered to himself. "Come on, buddy. If anyone can get out of this, it's you. Don't give up on me now."

The port wing dipped as Lawson came in and scraped the ground. Michael roared as the plane spun around. The wing detached from the rest of the aircraft, and the cockpit smashed into the ground 300 yards from where he was standing. A horrible igniting sound filled the air as the remaining fuel in the tanks caught fire.

Without realizing it, Michael found himself running headlong to the wreck. Fire had engulfed the plane, and he could hear the screams from the cockpit as he got closer. He ran toward the sounds. One of the firemen tackled him and wouldn't let him go.

"Stay back. That thing's about to blow. The other gas tank —"

The explosion cut off his words. The airplane split apart, engulfed in a massive fireball that knocked both Michael and the fireman who had saved him off their feet.

Michael sprang up again in an instant. He could feel the heat of the flames wash over his face. "Lawson!" he screamed. But the only sound from the cockpit now was the flames consuming the metal and cracking the glass. He fell to his knees as Captain Thomas arrived beside him.

The firemen moved in with foam and water, but there was little to be done other than let it burn out. Uncontrollable grief overtook Michael's body, and tears poured down his face, his head in his hands. He'd seen death in training before, but not like this. Captain Thomas pulled him to his feet.

"It's over," the instructor said. "Let the firefighters do their job."

Michael looked around him in despair. Perhaps Lawson had somehow escaped. A dozen other recruits stood in a circle behind him, looking on in shock at the fading inferno.

Captain Hart appeared and put his arm around Michael's shoulders. "I'm sorry about your friend. Captain Jansen was a friend of mine too."

"He had a wife and three kids," Michael said. "All he wanted was to serve his country."

"And he died doing just that. There's no difference between the men who die in training and those we lose in combat. We're all part of the same brotherhood. Nothing will ever change that."

The sun faded over the horizon as Hart led him back to the barracks. Other men offered him their condolences as he sat on the lower bunk, the one he and Lawson had tossed a coin over only two days ago. But few dwelled on what had just happened. They'd all seen death before. He could hear them counting it up in low voices. It seemed Lawson was the sixth recruit they had flown with to die.

"It wasn't his fault. He was a good flyer," one of them said to Michael. "He was brave. There's no shame."

Michael thanked him without being sure what he was thanking him for. He needed to talk to Monika. He needed his wife. He needed her here to comfort him. Writing would have to do. He searched through his pack for paper and pencil and wrote two sides, telling her of his friend and how he'd died. But when he'd finished, he crumpled it up and wrote a different letter instead, a cheerful one, saying how everything was fine and how much he longed to see her again and asking her to write soon. He addressed the letter to the OSS training camp in

Maryland and left the barracks to put it in the mailbox by the office.

Sleep didn't come easily that night. The base was silent, and somewhere in the distance, he heard an owl screeching in the darkness.

5

Monika was awake before the drill instructor came in to roar at them. As the only woman in the training camp, she had her own section of the newly constructed barracks to herself. The powers that be had hung a curtain around her bunk to preserve her dignity, but she could still hear the men's snores at night.

The window beside her bed revealed a gray, rainy morning, and Monika cursed under her breath. Shipley, the drill instructor, relished these days. The wetter and colder it was, the more he made them run—especially her.

Sure enough, he had a broad smile on his face as she lined up with the other recruits for the morning call. "Well, if it isn't our princess," he said, stalking over to her as she stood in the middle of the line.

Shipley was a wiry man in his early 40s with thinning hair. He was only an inch or two taller than Monika but made up for his lack of height with sheer force of will. She kept her eyes forward as he pushed his face into hers.

"You feel like running this morning, little lady?" He was so close to her that she could smell the coffee on his breath.

"I'm ready, sir," she said.

"Because if you don't feel like it—if your feet are too delicate, or you don't want to mess up your hair, you can quit. All you have to do is say the word, and I'll drive you to the bus station myself."

"I'm not going anywhere, sir."

Monika had been at the training camp in the Catoctin Forest for two weeks, and Shipley had asked her when she was quitting several times a day. He had asked her more than all the other 20 men in the barracks with her put together. His constant questioning of her commitment and fitness to be there had caused her to ponder whether she should return to her comfortable apartment in New York and try harder to get a job in one of the hundreds of factories popping up or being transformed from civilian to military use. Especially as she was currently being coached to speak English without an accent, which meant she might be able to disguise her German heritage.

But those moments of doubt disappeared in the night, and she woke every morning as determined as the day before to complete this course. If Shipley truly wanted her to quit, he wasn't going to succeed. His insults and epithets only steeled her determination to prove him wrong, if nothing else. She wasn't about to let this man get the better of her.

The recruits were lined up and followed the drill instructor out into the rain. Monika remained in the middle of the group. They started up through a rough path through the trees. Shipley's was the only voice they heard through the driving rain. He dropped back beside Monika, shouldering her, getting in her way, and slowing her up as the rest of the recruits ran past her unhindered.

"There's no place for spoiled little girls in my section," he growled. "Why don't you do us both a favor and end this? What are you going to do when you run into a Gestapo agent, smile at him, flutter your eyelashes?"

She didn't answer or even look at him. The only thing on her mind was placing one foot in front of the other. All that mattered was finishing the run. She knew he was doing one of two things—either he genuinely wanted her to drop out, or he was trying to toughen her up. If the first option was his true intention, he was going to be disappointed. Nothing this man or this training course could throw at her would be as difficult as losing her mother or having her father taken away by Gestapo thugs in the middle of the night. She could take whatever he could dish out and more. If it was the second option he was after, it was working.

Shipley stood on her foot, and this time, Monika stopped running and faced him. The other recruits disappeared around the corner. They still had more than three miles to go.

"Why are you doing this?" she said, looking calmly at the instructor. Keeping her face expressionless.

"I thought I'd made myself clear, little girl. You don't belong here." Something had gotten into him today. He'd never been this bad with her before.

Monika held his eyes for a moment longer, then sprinted on. Shipley caught up but didn't direct any more abuse at her as he ran past. Monika joined the back of the group and kept away from the instructor for the rest of the run. Just like the rain, she told herself, this would pass.

She was last to the breakfast table after her freezing shower.

"Shipley has it in for you, huh?" Bob Gillespie, a fellow recruit from Philadelphia, said to her in his posh voice. Like many other wannabe spies, he was from a well-to-do family. If the war hadn't come along, he would have been working at his father's law firm. The fledgling OSS was full of upper-class patriots like him. Some already said the acronym stood for 'Oh

So Snobby,' rather than the Office of Strategic Services. The top brass had recruited their friends' sons and daughters. Many of the other men had recruitment stories similar to Monika's about meeting someone at a ball or an upscale party in a mansion in the Hamptons. But few had a childhood like hers, not that they would know it; she'd shared nothing with them.

"I don't know what I ever did to him," Monika answered as she took her place.

"Maybe in a previous life," he said, and she smiled and shrugged.

Despite not being from the upper classes, she didn't feel too alone here. And she wasn't the only foreigner at the table. Two men sat at the end, speaking Czech. There were also a couple of Frenchmen and three Poles. She was the only German, but no one treated her any differently because of it. Some of them seemed to share Shipley's attitude toward her, but not because of her nationality, because she was a woman.

"Never mind Shipley," Gillespie said in his East Coast drawl. "I heard we're getting a new instructor this afternoon."

Breakfast was followed by two hours of gymnastics instruction—an area where even Shipley couldn't deny Monika's prowess. Then, her group was taken to a classroom where they sat through some lectures on personal disguise, observation, and communications. After class, when the other recruits went to lunch, Monika went to a separate prefab, where her own particular instructor awaited. This had become her favorite hour of the day. Mrs. Patricia Kerner, a retired voice actor who'd starred in some radio plays she'd listened to in the past, sat waiting for her.

"Hello, Monika," the older woman said. Her blonde hair fell below her shoulders. It was comforting to talk to a civilian every day, and she was the only one who enjoyed the privilege.

"Hi, Patricia," she replied in her sunniest California accent.

The voice coach smiled. "Very good. Have you been practicing?"

"Every day."

"Have you any idea why they hired you to do this for me yet?" Monika asked as she sat down. A copy of *Of Mice and Men* was on the table.

"They still haven't told me," Patricia replied. "And I don't expect they will, either. In the meantime, you and I have a job to do. The one thing I will say is that they've definitely got a specific purpose in mind. They wouldn't bring me all the way out here for nothing. Now, let's read."

Monika dismissed thoughts of why she was doing this and picked up the book, focusing on each word as she read it aloud.

Monika joined the rest of the cadets an hour later, and they met the new man Gillespie had referred to at breakfast. The rain had given way, and it was a fine sunny afternoon. The recruits sat on bleachers in front of a clearing in the trees as a tall, muscular man with a deep tan stood before them.

"My name is Dan Albarn," the new instructor said in an English accent. "So far, you've been taught small arms and rifle training. You've been shown the basics of mortars and explosives and even had the chance to fire a bazooka, if I'm not wrong."

Monika smiled to herself; she had enjoyed firing the bazooka at dumpsters set up to resemble German tanks.

"What you've learned up to this point is all very well. All very valuable. But I'm here to show you how to survive if you come toe to toe with a six-foot fanatical SS man who's been training to destroy you since he was nine years old. I'm here to teach you a hundred different ways to disable or kill an enemy before he can do that to you. You can kill with your hands, your feet, a knife, a pen, a rock—whatever is at hand, you have to know how to use it. Forget about fighting fair. In war, it's kill or be killed. Nothing else matters. May I have a volunteer from the recruits, please?"

Several threw their hands up. Albarn chose Vincent Lato, a Pole from Chicago—the biggest man from their barracks and someone who wanted to kill Nazis so badly that he rarely spoke about anything else.

Albarn stood opposite him. "Try to hit me," the Englishman said.

Lato laughed and threw a punch. Albarn bent back to dodge it, but before Lato could pull his arm back, the instructor grabbed his forearm and dug his fingers into his wrist. Lato buckled in pain and fell to his knees. Albarn raised his fist to punch him but stopped himself. He patted the recruit on the shoulder and sent him back to his seat.

"It doesn't matter how big they are," Albarn said. "Every man has the same weaknesses. If you know how to exploit them, you can beat them."

Monika was absorbed, and Albarn seemed to notice and called her up. "I think everyone could agree that I'm bigger than my friend here. But she might have something I'm not expecting. What's your name?" he asked.

Monika coughed, her hand to her chest; the words she tried to say were lost. Albarn tilted his head and asked again. She leaned in to tell him, still coughing. He brought his ear down to hear her. Seeing her chance, she brought her hand up and grabbed his throat, pushing her thumb hard into his jugular. Albarn was still able to escape, but once he did, the instructor stood back with a broad smile. He pointed at her. "I think you and I are going to get along just fine. What's your name?"

"Monika Ritter."

"Pleased to meet you, Miss Ritter."

"Mrs. Ritter."

He laughed before continuing the lesson.

Monika had heard of martial arts before and had even seen

some boys in the Hitler Youth attempt them back in the 30s, but she'd never seen an expert like Albarn perform it. He moved with a grace and speed she'd never witnessed. After class ended, she approached the Englishman. She didn't salute or treat him like she imagined Michael would have to treat his superiors. The atmosphere was different. There were few distinctions between the officers and the enlisted men and women. The stated aim of this camp was to produce toughened individuals with responsibility and initiative. There was no room for the mindless discipline of the other branches of the armed forces.

"I need your training more than most," she said. "I'm 30 pounds lighter than the next smallest recruit in my barracks."

"We had an old saying in Streatham when I was growing up —it's not the size of the dog in the fight, it's the size of the fight in the dog. When I'm finished with you, you'll be hard as granite, Ritter. I can see the desire in your eyes. That's all I need to mold you. I'm not worried about you at all."

They walked back to the mess hall together.

"You see this?" Albarn said, drawing a double-edged fighting knife from a scabbard. It had a foil grip and a thin, pointed blade. He placed it in Monika's hand. "I designed this myself based on my experiences. It's ideal for the quick, vicious combat you'll be forced to use when you're behind the lines, and I will make you an expert with it. If you remember nothing else from your time with me, realize that if you're going to survive, you'll need to get tough. Get down in the gutter and win at all costs."

Monika smiled and handed back the dagger. "You ever get the urge to get on the boat to Europe yourself?"

"At my age?" he said, chuckling and shaking his head. "I'll leave the combat to youngsters like you. Just remember what I teach you over the next few weeks, and you'll be fine."

Two nights later, Monika was woken in the middle of the night by Albarn's voice; she jerked upright in the dark.

"Time to go, Ritter," the Englishman said in a low voice. "Duty calls. Get dressed." He pushed back the curtain around her bunk and walked away.

He was waiting outside by a jeep with the engine running when she emerged from the barracks. The headlights pierced the night and highlighted the raindrops falling through. Monika climbed into the passenger's seat and was thrust back against the leather as he pushed down on the gas.

"What's this about?" she asked, but Albarn didn't answer. Somehow, he knew where he was going in the darkness, straight past the main camp to a new building Monika hadn't seen before. That was no surprise; the place was under constant construction. More and more recruits were arriving every day. She wasn't even the only woman anymore. Several others had arrived in the past few days. She wondered if Shipley was as hard on them as he'd been on her.

The bungalow was at least 50 feet long. Monika couldn't make out where it ended but could see it was made of logs cut from the forest. A lantern outside the door was the only light apart from the jeep's headlamps.

Albarn reached into a bag in the back of the jeep and pulled out a .45 and two clips. "There's a Nazi soldier inside the house," he said. "Go in and kill him."

Monika knew not to ask unnecessary questions and slammed the clip into the pistol.

"Two bullets, remember!" her instructor reminded her as she approached the door.

She nodded. She fully subscribed to all of Albarn's methods, chief of which was the principle of firing two quick shots at the enemy before they had a chance to adjust.

Apart from that, she had no idea what awaited her as she tried the door. It was locked. She kicked it in and found herself in a long, dimly lit hallway with doors on each side. The only sound she could hear was that of her heart pounding in her chest. She held the gun in both hands. One of the doors opened in front of her, and she fell to her knees to fire two bullets into the paper-target Nazi soldier. Another German SS man popped up at the end of the hall, and she did the same thing. She whirled around, saw what seemed like a French resistance figure, and held her fire. She ran toward another target at the end of the hallway and took it down before slamming the other clip into the gun. She heard the sound of German crowds at a Nazi rally. Hitler's voice carried through the hallways. She kicked open another door and fired twice at another Wehrmacht trooper, missing the second shot. That room led into another. She could sense Albarn behind her, but he remained silent. The sound of the baying crowd grew louder as she approached what she hoped was the final door. She pulled it open, and a rope attached to a pulley turned an armchair with a dummy of Adolf Hitler in it. She pumped her last two shots into his chest and ejected the magazine from her weapon.

"Check your sidearm," Albarn said.

She did as she was told before handing it to him.

"Impressive, Ritter," he said with a smile. "You missed one shot but took that Nazi down anyway. I knew you'd amount to something the first moment I laid eyes on you."

Monika couldn't hide the elation surging through her.

"Why haven't I heard about this place before?" she asked.

"Because you're the first to use it. Construction only finished this afternoon. You like the touch with Hitler at the end?"

"Very much," she answered with a beaming smile.

As the weeks wore on, training became a grueling marathon. The recruits fired more weapons than Monika had ever known – American, British, and German guns – and learned to strip and clean all of them. Monika and her fellow recruits crawled through rain-soaked oak forests in the dead of night to plant live demolition charges on floodlit sheds, all while evading the other recruits who were on sentry duty there. In their few spare moments, they were taught secret radio procedures and practiced typing out code and encrypting messages. And all the while, she continued her elocution lessons. Most mornings began with a run. Shipley still supervised these and didn't let up with his bullying tactics but at least spread them more evenly among the recruits, not focusing solely on Monika anymore. A new obstacle course was constructed to complement the training with real explosive charges under the rope bridges and wire catwalks. The recruits crawled under razor wire with live rounds whistling above their heads. After three months, only 11 of the original 20 remained in Monika's barracks. Seven had resigned. Two had died. Much to Shipley's frustration, the German girl was not one of the former.

The recruits left the forest only to learn parachute jumping, and as well as mastering the basics of the freefall, they were taught how to dispose of the chute and what to do if they were seen or got caught in trees while descending. Monika saw and felt her body transform into a walking weapon. It was as if the instructors had seen who she was underneath and sculpted her from stone.

She was lying on her bunk, reading another cheerful letter from Michael, when Gemma Anderson, her new bunkmate, came to find her.

"You're wanted in the meeting room," she said.

"Okay," Monika replied. She kissed the paper and folded it back into the envelope to finish later.

Michael had completed his training in the AT-10s and was ready to graduate to the bombers that he would fly on missions. He had requested the biggest, most technologically advanced airplane the US Army Air Force had to offer—the Flying Fortress. She would have liked to read to the end, where he always told her how much he loved her, but she knew her instructors wouldn't take kindly to being kept waiting.

Albarn and Shipley were in the meeting room with Gillespie and two other recruits she'd trained with since the beginning. The instructors were standing in front of a blackboard with the trainees facing them, and Shipley motioned to the spare chair at the front as she walked in.

"Take a seat, Ritter," he growled. "And listen to your instructions."

"Time to take the next step," Albarn began, with a friendlier look. "We've hidden a package in a factory in Baltimore, and let me tell you, it won't be easy getting it out."

"What is it?" a recruit from Tampa called Wilson asked.

"Irrelevant," Albarn answered. "Your task is to retrieve it. Nothing else. It's small enough for one person to carry."

"Security in the building is tight," Shipley said. "As far as the guards there will be concerned, you'll be nothing more than common burglars. It'll be your job to sneak past them and stay out of jail."

"We've had incidents with trainees where they got caught by the police or the FBI and spent the night in jail. Don't let that happen to you," Albarn said. "You need to pass this test to graduate." He turned to the board. "Your target is the radio factory in Canton. The package is in a safe in the factory manager's office on the third floor. This is the address." Albarn wrote it on the board. "Memorize it."

Shipley picked up a pile of papers from a desk beside him and handed one to each trainee. "These are rough plans for the layout of the factory—the type you might get from an asset in the field."

Monika examined the map of the building in her hand. It was blurred out in parts and blank at the back of the building, but the manager's office was clearly marked at the front of the building on the third floor. The safe was marked in the corner.

"How do we get into the safe? Do we try to find the combination?"

Shipley snorted and rolled his eyes. "It's not going to be written down in his diary, Ritter."

Albarn was more charitable with his words. "Just take whatever you need from our storeroom or our armory. You have been put together with deliberate care. Each of you has a certain set of skills that we've recognized. If you can work as a team, you will succeed. If you act as individuals, you'll fall apart." He rubbed the address off the board. "Take a few minutes to talk it over. It's 19:35 now. Leave by 22:00. The guards change shifts at midnight. We'll leave the planning to you. Remember your training."

The instructors walked out, leaving silence behind them. Monika was the first to speak. "We need a truck and a way to get into that safe."

"A truck isn't a problem," said Miles Rowan, a former minor league baseball player who had been expected to rise to the majors until the war intervened. "The keys are on the wall in the barracks."

"And I can get into that safe with a PETN plastic explosive," said Wilson.

"That will make a hell of a bang. And what if you blow the safe to smithereens?" worried Gillespie.

"Trust me," Wilson answered. "This is my specialty. Yes, it will be loud, but I won't blow the thing apart. While the rest of you have been off socializing, I've been spending all my spare time with the explosives. Trust me."

"I have a rule never to trust anyone who says 'trust me,'" Monika said, not entirely joking. She stood up and found a piece of chalk by the blackboard. "We're going to need a driver and a lookout. The others go inside for the package."

"What if we run into a guard?" Wilson said.

"I don't want to use any of Albarn's fighting skills on some retired cop working at night to supplement his pension. Our best option is not getting caught, but if we do, we'll have to take our night or two in jail. Albarn and Shipley will get us out. They won't want to lose us after all the time and resources they've put in," Monika replied.

The recruits spent the next few minutes reviewing the plan as Monika wrote up a quick set of bullet points. The sticking point was the explosive – it would be hard to get out fast enough after a bang like that. Monika thought they should look around for a clue to the combination, despite what Shipley had said; the others were anxious about spending too much time in there.

"We'll do our best with what we have," she summarized after a few minutes of heated discussion. "I think we agree that speed is the most important element. Wilson can set up the explosive while I hunt for the combination, and whoever gets there first..."

Once she was satisfied that they'd done all they could to be prepared, she rubbed the board clean, and the trainees returned to the barracks to change into black clothes with matching ski masks.

Rowan procured the truck, and by 22:00 hours, they were

ready to go. Neither instructor came to wish them luck. Rowan pulled out of the camp and drove down the dark forest roads toward the highway.

It was a two-hour drive to Baltimore. The road was quiet for the first 90 minutes, although they saw more cars as they reached the outskirts of the city. The talk of gas rationing hadn't come to anything yet, and people still drove just as much as before.

It felt strange to Monika to be out and about once more. She hadn't left the camp in almost three months. Some of the others had gotten out briefly to see family, but with her husband undergoing training of his own, she hadn't seen the point in interrupting her instructions. Now that she was out in the city, albeit only in the front cabin of a truck, she wished she had taken the opportunity. It was a Friday night—something that didn't matter in the camp, but outside in places like this, life still went on. Lovers walked hand in hand on the streets, and soldiers and sailors swelled the bars before they shipped out.

This flirtation with regular life was a brief one. Rowan continued through to the industrial section of Canton, in the southeast of the city. They drove down darkened streets and saw few people. Everything was shuttered for the night. Monika had heard of some factories working 24 hours a day, churning out planes and munitions for the war effort, but that wasn't the case here.

"This is it," Monika said as they pulled up outside another darkened, nondescript-looking factory. "The gates are locked. Pull in the alley beside."

Rowan did as he was told. Monika jumped out of the cabin and went to the back of the truck.

"We're going to need the bolt cutters," she told Wilson. "Get us in, then I'll take care of the lock on the door."

"Won't be a problem," he responded.

Gillespie stood at the entrance to the alley, looking up and down the street. He was the designated lookout. Rowan's part of the plan was to stay in the truck, ready to leave if the others came running. Gillespie gave a low owl hoot to signal that the coast was clear, and then he, Monika, and Wilson ran around to the gate.

Wilson was as good as his word and made quick work of the padlock. They ran through the parking lot out front and made it to the wall by a side door just as the glare of a flashlight illuminated the night. Monika dived behind a massive dumpster, followed by the others, and they crouched in the dark as the nightwatchman sauntered past. He stopped in full view of them, lit a cigarette, threw the match in the dumpster, and kept walking. They waited until his footsteps turned the corner before crawling out again.

Gillespie ran to the corner to watch out for the watchman coming around again. The building was a square, and each side was at least 200 yards long, so they had maybe fifteen minutes.

"Can you get through that lock?" Wilson whispered to Monika as they reached the side door.

"Piece of cake."

She took a lock-picking kit from the satchel on her shoulder. Despite the moon above, it was dark in the yard, but she'd done this so many times that when it came time for the real thing, she could have picked the lock with her eyes closed. It was an old-fashioned bolt lock—no problem. She pushed the door open, and she and Wilson moved inside, closing it behind them.

It was even darker inside, but they didn't want to use the small flashlights they carried because of the long windows. Monika pictured the simple map of the interior of the factory in her mind and led the way to the stairwell at the edge of the factory floor. They crept up three flights of stairs and down a darkened hallway, using their little flashlights now. The factory manager's office was locked, but although this door took a little longer than the first, Monika got through it in seconds. The light of the moon and stars poured into the small office through the large plate glass windows, and they switched off their flashlights. Wilson hurried over to the safe in the corner. It was about three feet high and about two feet deep. It had a black dial on the front to enter the code and looked impenetrable.

Monika searched for clues as he set up the PETN plastic explosive he'd brought, with wires and a fuse.

The manager's desk was illuminated in silver moonlight. It was clean and tidy, with the papers piled neatly in the corner. In the corner was a framed photo of the factory manager holding a massive fish with a little girl.

"Wait," Monika said suddenly as Wilson completed his preparations. "Just give me a minute." She started hunting through the desk.

"Wait for what? We don't have much time," Wilson hissed. "That nightwatchman will be back around any second, and who knows if any of his buddies are in here."

"Just give me a minute…" Here was the manager's diary, and in the front, on a designated page, was a list of important events of the year: a wedding anniversary, Mother's Day, and Evangeline's 8th birthday party.

"Come on!" Wilson begged.

"Just let me try this one combination." She hurried over, and her fingers flew around the dial. 052034. The safe creaked open.

Wilson was beside himself with glee. "How on earth did you know?"

"His daughter's birthday."

"Looks like we passed the test!"

"So far. We're not home yet. Take the explosive away. We don't want this little girl's father blowing himself up in the morning."

"Okay, okay." As he dismantled the little homemade bomb, she took out the package, which was wrapped in brown paper and tied with string. It had a note on it that read, "take me."

"I wonder what's in here," Wilson grinned.

"Are you ready? Let's go." She tucked the package under her arm and closed the safe.

Gillespie was waiting for them outside.

"Let's go," he whispered. "The nightwatchman just turned down the near side."

They kept low as they ran softly to the gate. Monika tried to temper the exhilaration surging through her. Was this the last test before graduation? Rowan started the truck's engine as they ran around the corner into the alley. She leaped into the cabin as the others threw themselves into the back.

6

Gillespie and Rowan were already sitting in the debriefing room when Monika arrived. Monika greeted her fellow recruits and took a seat around the table. Gillespie asked how they were doing after the mission the night before, but there wasn't time for an answer. The door opened, and all four stood as Albarn and Shipley entered. In keeping with the atmosphere of the camp, the cadets sat down again without saluting.

Albarn was the first to speak. "Last night's mission was a success, I hear."

"We retrieved the package, sir," Rowan said.

Shipley scowled, seemingly unable to say something positive about a mission that had gone without a hitch.

"I'm sure you're aware that there won't be any graduation ceremony," Albarn stated with a half-smile. "But know that we're pleased with each one of you. Even my friend here." He clapped Shipley on the shoulder, and he responded with a simple nod. It was the friendliest gesture she'd ever seen from him.

Albarn had a manilla folder with him, and he opened it. "I'm sure you're all very eager to find out your assignments."

Monika and the two recruits looked at each other in anticipation. What the Englishman revealed in the next few seconds would shape their subsequent lives. Monika wanted Switzerland, and Mr. Dulles was already there.

Albarn drew out a piece of paper. "Gillespie, you're being assigned to London. Rowan, you're off to Lisbon, and Ritter, you're staying here for now, in the good old US of A."

"What?" Monika asked.

"There's more, Ritter. Just wait," Albarn said and leaned forward. "Your first assignment is to infiltrate a group of Nazi spies we believe are operating in America. Have you any experience meeting anyone you might have determined to be a threat to national security, Ritter?"

"In my life here?" Monika replied. "Only members of the German American Bund."

Monika had been an accidental attendee at the zenith of the American Nazis in Madison Square Garden before the war started, but the organization had collapsed once the fighting began in 1939. The men she'd seen that night in New York were nothing more than flag-bearing followers. The same as the people who attended the hysterical mass rallies in Germany. They'd never have the audacity to try to strike against the government on US soil. The German American Bund, the predominant Nazi group in the States, was illegal now. This was something different. She had heard of Nazi agents in America. There had been stories in the newspapers about sabotage at the docks in New York and Baltimore. Perhaps this Nazi cell was to blame.

"Are they the ones responsible for those ships being bombed? Was that them?" she asked.

"That's what we want you to find out, Mrs. Ritter," Albarn said, reaching into the folder. He pushed a photograph taken from a distance, of a man walking into a bar. "We have reason to believe this man is one of the men we're searching for."

Monika took the picture in her hand. "Where and when was this taken?"

"Last week at a bar in Baltimore. The man's name is Manfred Paulitz. He's a factory worker in the city and frequents the bar every Thursday and Friday night. He's been overheard spouting some inflammatory rhetoric in the past, and some men have been listening in to his radio transmissions. We think he might be in contact with Germany."

"You're not sure?" Monika inquired.

"The transmissions stopped a couple of weeks ago. That's when we thought of you. Your job will be to meet the man and gain his confidence. The fact that you're a woman won't harm your cause."

"When?" Monika asked.

"It's Thursday today, isn't it?" Shipley growled.

"You ready for tonight? Albarn asked.

Monika replied with a nod. "I'll need to get something to wear."

"I'm sure we can arrange that," Albarn responded.

"What if he doesn't approach me?" she asked. "Am I just going to walk up to him?"

Albarn shook his head. "We have a cover story. He deals with hiring in the factory he works in. Tell him you heard he was the man to see about a job."

Monika nodded and began to mentally prepare herself for what was to come.

Monika borrowed a car from the training camp and drove into Baltimore after lunch. After several surreal hours of clothes shopping in the city, she checked into a hotel and changed into her new dress. She applied just enough makeup to make herself presentable, stopping short of being alluring. She was a married woman, and there were certain lines she wouldn't cross. People had been acting differently since the war began. No one knew who would live or die, and many seemed to have forgotten the traditional morality that had reigned her whole life up until now. If the OSS expected her to fraternize with this man in that regard, they had another thing coming. Monika applied a little red lipstick and took one last look at herself as she smacked her lips together.

"You can do this," she said to the woman staring back at her in the mirror.

Monika had dinner alone and then walked through the working-class neighborhood of Federal Hill. Dunphy's, a dive bar on the corner of Battery Avenue and West Street, was dark as she entered. The walls were covered in old photographs of lush rural landscapes. An Irish flag hung on the wall behind the bar, but the sound of men speaking German and Czech at the tables by the door betrayed the mixed nature of the bar and the city itself. She took a seat alone, wary of men's eyes. The place smelled faintly of stale beer. It was as if no matter how many times the floors were scrubbed, the odor remained. The bartender, a man in his 30s with a flat cap and a thin black beard, rested muscular forearms on the bar as he addressed her.

"What'll it be?"

"Natural Bohemian," she responded.

He grinned and fetched the bottle for her. It was a local beer and would go some way toward showing she wasn't a fish out of water here.

The bartender returned with the drink. "Never seen you in here before."

"I'm looking for someone. You know Manfred Paulitz?"

"Don't know him. Lots of Germans in this neighborhood now, though."

Surprised that the bartender didn't know Manfred, Monika smiled and settled back in her seat. She scanned the room and was watching the door as Manfred walked in five minutes later. He walked down to the end of the bar where she was sitting. He was tall and lean with short brown hair and a handsome, chiseled face. Monika took a drink and turned to him.

"I'm looking for someone."

He looked across at her with surprise. She saw the attraction in his eyes and knew she had him.

"How can I help you?"

"You know Manfred Paulitz?"

A bright smile spread across his face. "I'd say so. I'm Manfred."

Monika laughed with her hand over her mouth. "Oh, wow! It must be my lucky day." Though she was proud of the mid-Atlantic American accent she had learned in training, it was dispelled for her natural German brogue.

"I'm Greta," she chuckled and shook his hand. "I just arrived in Baltimore from New York. I heard you're the man to speak to about a job."

He ordered a drink and sat down. They spoke for a few minutes about the box factory he worked in. "I can get you something. How long are you in the city for?"

Monika shrugged. "I'm living with my aunt and uncle in Towson. I'll see."

Manfred nodded and ordered them both another beer.

"Do you like living in America?" she asked.

"Sometimes," he responded as he stared at the colorful liquor bottles lined up behind the bar.

"What do you mean?"

"We've all been living here in America for years now, and we know how the average person on the street treats honorable

German citizens. We've all felt it, but more importantly, we see the hypocrisy of Roosevelt and the American politicians who profess to fight for freedom. We're very much aware that the opposite is true.

"Who is 'we'?"

"Germans like you."

"Like me?"

"How long have you been in the country, Greta?"

"I came here in '39."

"And you've taken to life in the United States?"

Monika nodded. "In the main, yes."

Manfred narrowed his eyes. "Would you say the Americans are welcoming to foreigners?"

"I used to live in New York. Almost everyone I meet is a foreigner. This is an immigrant nation."

"Except for when it's not. Do you find the native-born Americans to be hospitable to Germans?" Monika didn't answer. Manfred continued. "What about since the war began? Have you suffered abuse from strangers on the street when they heard your accent?"

"On occasion."

"What do you think is better about the United States? How is it superior to the Reich in your mind?"

Monika took a second to gather her thoughts. The rapport between them was growing.

"I'm not sure. It seems more prosperous."

"For some, perhaps, but the Great Depression lasted a lot longer here than in Germany. Hitler saw to that. Some people can vote here, yes, but what of the disenfranchised black population in the South? This country was founded on lies, and they are the bedrock it still functions on. Hitler is forthright in his beliefs. He trusts the German people enough to tell them the truth. He keeps the promises he makes. I'm sure you've heard about the internment camps set up to house the innocent

Japanese population. Look around this country with open eyes, and you'll see hypocrisy everywhere."

Monika suppressed the anger burning inside her. She wanted to ask him about the concentration camps where innocent people perceived as enemies of the state died every day. Where her father had perished.

"No system or place is perfect."

"You're right, Greta. Absolutely correct. And just like the American system has its faults, so does the National Socialist one. I don't pretend for a moment that everything the Nazi government enacts on a daily basis is perfect, but I do know that it's best for the Reich. The curse of democracy has been vanquished, and the German people are much the better without it."

"Do you think America would do better under National Socialism?"

"I'm sure of it. Perhaps one day, when the American people fully understand the benefits of National Socialism, they'll institute it here. What a day that would be!"

Monika wanted to advise him not to hold his breath while he waited for that to happen but just nodded along with his sentiment instead.

"Yes," Manfred continued. "You and I are very similar people. We're both from the same country. We share a passion to make a difference in this world in the brief time we have here and have the determination to act upon our ambitions."

They finished their drinks at the same time. Manfred looked around. "I live close by. Perhaps we should go to my apartment. We can speak freely there."

Monika took a second before she nodded. It didn't feel strange to agree to his request. She was entirely in character now.

Manfred paid for their drinks and led her outside. Several

men stared at her as she went. It was dark outside, and Monika buttoned her coat to stave off the cold.

"Don't worry, it's not far," he said.

They walked down the street and around the corner to the third door in a line of rowhouses. He took a key from his pocket and opened the door. The living room was clean. It looked barely lived in. She took a seat in an armchair. Manfred went to the kitchen, brought back two bottles of beer, and sat opposite her.

After a few seconds, he went to the phonograph in the corner and put on a record. Wagner's *Ride of the Valkyries* began.

"One of our Führer's favorites," he said.

"And mine," Monika exclaimed with enthusiasm.

They talked about the job for a few minutes before Manfred took the Wagner record off the phonograph and replaced it with another. A few seconds later, Hitler's shrill voice began.

"These are existential times for the German people," the dictator said. "We are facing unprecedented threats on many fronts, but none is greater than the lurking menace of Bolshevism."

Manfred sat on the couch as the record played. Monika tried to block it out while pretending to listen, but Hitler's voice had a hypnotic ring. It was almost impossible to ignore.

"If men wish to live, they are forced to kill others," the dictator continued. "The entire struggle for survival is a conquest of the means of existence which in turn means eliminating others from these same sources of subsistence. As long as there are people on this earth, there will be nations against nations, and they will be forced to protect their vital rights in the same way as the individual is forced to protect his own. One is either the hammer or the anvil. It is our responsibility to prepare the German people for the role of the hammer."

Monika recognized the sentiments. It was an old speech, preparing the listeners for the state of war Hitler was to launch them into. Monika remembered people at the time dismissing the Führer's ideas as nonsense, but he was explicit in his intentions. He'd told the German people and the rest of the world exactly what he intended to do. People, and particularly the leaders of the opposing European powers, had only really sat up to listen when he began carrying out the plans he'd warned them of in advance.

Monika sat for about 15 minutes, suffering Hitler's ramblings about power and the inherent greatness of the German people.

"What do you think of the Führer's speeches?" Manfred asked.

"He's an impressive speaker. I sometimes wonder who he might have been if he'd directed his energies differently."

"Is there a better cause to adopt than the betterment of a nation? But you're right. With his talents, Hitler could have been the richest man in the world. He could have dominated the commercial world, but he chose a different path. He lives a frugal life. He has one goal—one obsession. It truly is a privilege to serve him. All my colleagues are of the same mind."

"To serve him?" Monika asked.

"In a way, yes. Does that surprise you?"

"It's good to give yourself to something that feels greater than yourself."

Manfred put down his beer bottle and leaned forward. "I'm from Munich," he began. "My father came back a cripple from the Great War. A shell landed in his trench. He was the only man around him who survived, but he lost an arm, and his left leg below the knee. I hardly recognized him when he came home. I was just a boy but old enough to remember the handsome, vibrant man my father had been. The man who returned to us was a hideous monster with scars all across his face. He was a carpenter before the war—a wonderful craftsman. Our house was beautiful, with ornate wooden carvings everywhere.

He built it himself, but the shell ended all that for him. He came home to a country in turmoil with no prospects. My mother found enough work to feed me and my three sisters while he searched for a way forward. The government wanted nothing to do with him. Most of the disabled veterans ended up dead or on the street. But one man introduced him to a different way. A fledgling organization had begun on the streets of Munich—an organization for the neglected, forgotten patriots in German society. It wasn't just for the heroes the new democratic government had left behind; it was run by them. He began to attend meetings in beerhouses with his new friends and was soon introduced to an inspirational young firebrand who had served with distinction on the Western Front. That man imbued everyone who met him with a source of pride and hope that Germany could once again become one of the world's great nations. That man was Adolf Hitler."

"That's amazing."

Manfred ignored her comment. "My father was a changed man. The country was still in turmoil, reeling from the effects of unfettered liberal democracy, but through Hitler and his teachings, he found direction and purpose. He picked himself up and began working as a carpenter again."

"With one arm and one leg?"

"Yes. With Hitler as his inspiration, nothing could stop him. And it wasn't just my father, either. That young man lifted hundreds, then thousands of men up by their bootstraps just through his words. My father joined the party in the early days and was there among the true patriots in '23 for the Beer Hall Putsch. He was so convinced that Hitler was the only man to carry Germany forward that he put his life on the line. A bullet skimmed his coat that day. He was just behind Hitler when a policeman almost shot him and tended to Göring when he was wounded."

"Hitler was almost shot that day?"

"A bullet missed him by inches. How different history would have been if that policeman had shot straight."

"How different indeed."

Monika was interested in this man's motivations. She was prepared to listen to him and also evaluate the methods by which he intended to try to turn her sympathies to the Nazi cause.

"The Weimar criminals victimized Hitler for trying to change the direction of a failing country."

"It was my understanding that he was jailed for treason and given little more than a slap on the wrist," she answered.

"One man's treason is another man's heroism. Think of what Hitler was trying to do. His only motivation was to drag Germany out of the mud. Don't forget the state the country was in during those years."

"I was a little girl, but I remember. My parents tried to shield me from it, but even at that age, I recognized the stress I saw in them."

"Your parents, my parents. Everyone felt it. Hitler's obsession was with providing a better future for all loyal Germans."

She thought to ask him about the word "loyal" but wanted to seem more submissive and open to his ideas.

"My father stayed in the party. His fellow SA and National Socialist Party members became like brothers to him. He even brought me along to meet the Führer at a meeting after he was released from jail. I was only a boy at the time, but I still remember the feeling he engendered within me just by shaking my hand and looking me in the eye. I knew I was in the presence of a truly great man. I wasn't sure about my father's political leanings until that day, but I became just like him after that. I put on the uniform and began marching through the streets with the other patriots. I rose through the ranks and, in the fullness of time, joined the party myself. The day Hitler came to power was one of the happiest of my father's life. It was the culmination of years of hard work. The better future for Germany that he'd dedicated his life to, became a reality."

"Is he happy with Hitler's new Reich?"

"My father lived to see many of Hitler's accomplishments but died in '37. He was buried according to his wishes—in his SA uniform, draped in the new German flag."

"The swastika."

"He didn't live a long life. The rigors of the war were unescapable, but he died contented that he'd made a difference. It's my will to go the same way. Hitler and the National Socialist cause saved him from a life of misery and destitution. In the same way, the cause saved my family and thousands of others. Germany is unrecognizable from what it was when we were young. People have pride in their country now and have faith in the institutions that run it."

Monika knew that getting into an argument with this man would set her back and could even cost her her life. But still, it was so hard to hold her tongue.

"My work here is a continuation of his legacy," Manfred said. "His obsession has become mine. This war won't last forever, and when the final victory is complete, the world will be how he wanted it to be."

The record of Hitler's speech finished. Manfred walked over and turned it over. The cheers came first, then the despot's voice followed.

"What about your father? What kind of a man was he?"

She would have to take this slowly to remember all the details of her tall tale. "He was stubborn. We fought a lot. My father fought on the Western Front just like yours. He made it home in one piece but was a different man. According to my mother, anyway. I was too young back then to notice the difference. The man I grew up with was bitter and twisted, obsessed by what he deemed to be the unnecessary surrender to the Allies and the chaos that followed in his wake."

"We all lived through those miserable times. Many millions of loyal Germans felt the same way. Did you find yourself rebelling against your father because of his unpleasant manner?"

"He was impossible. He would come home drunk, looking to take out whatever was inside him on me or my poor mother. She tried to protect me, but sometimes she couldn't. One night back in '32, it got so bad I ran away, but I came back the next day. I couldn't leave my mother alone with him."

Manfred leaned forward, his hands clasped together, eager for her to continue. He seemed to be buying what she was selling him.

"What were his political beliefs?"

"He and his friends grasped onto the Nazi ideals as soon as they heard them. The National Socialist movement took longer to catch on in Berlin than in Munich, but my father was a staunch Nazi by the time of the election in '30 when they gained so many seats."

Monika thought back to the visit to her cousin's house in Ulm when her mother died. She decided to use Uncle Dieter as her model of who a dedicated Nazi would be, except for the fact that her uncle was still alive and well, serving his beloved Führer.

"He fell deeper and deeper in with the Nazis. He rose through the party and became a local supervisor, making sure others adhered to the National Socialist ideals."

"Did his drinking continue when he began working for the Reich?"

Monika shook her head. "He gave up completely. The last drink he had was when I was about 15."

"Perhaps he found purpose in the cause."

"If he did, it didn't improve our relationship," Monika said. "My mother didn't agree with his politics. It almost came between them. I don't know what would have happened if it wasn't for the accident."

"The accident?"

"He was killed in car crash in '36. He and two friends of his."

"What were their names?"

"Franz Weber and Helmut Klose. I didn't know them well. They were fellow party members. And then my mother died."

"It all makes sense now," he said.

"What does?"

"It explains why you came to America. Why you're hiding from the war. You blamed Hitler for your father's relationship with your mother, so in some ways, you connect the Führer to the death of your parents. But I don't think it's fair to blame all that on the National Socialist cause. It sounds to me that your father would have been worse off if he hadn't found meaning in his life through Hitler."

Monika took a few seconds to digest what he'd said. "Perhaps you're right."

"I am right, Greta. Why do you think your father found a home in the National Socialist movement?" he asked her.

She didn't answer. He remained silent. She was next to speak ten seconds later.

"I suppose it offered him a sense of belonging he hadn't felt since the war. His life was a mess, and Hitler's promises of order and a return to greatness must have been enticing."

"I'd say so, but don't forget about his deep love for the Fatherland. He served our country on the Western Front. He saw men sacrifice their lives for a government that didn't care about their comrades when they returned. Can you imagine how angry he must have been?"

"I don't have to imagine it. I saw it."

"He recognized the chance the National Socialists offered for Germany. And I think if he were here today, in this room, he'd be sitting beside me saying exactly what I've been saying to you."

"And what's that?"

"That there is a better way, and Herr Hitler has shown us the path to it. He's the best chance Germany will ever have."

Monika made sure to smile. "Perhaps you're right. I might need to put my personal issues aside. I would like to do my part to help the Fatherland, too, in any way I can." She stood up. "But it's time I got home. My aunt and uncle will be wondering where I am."

Manfred walked her to the door.

"I'll come to the factory next week," Monika said as he opened the door for her.

"Perhaps we can meet before then. There's a meeting of loyal, like-minded Germans tomorrow evening if you'd like to attend."

"I'd love to!" Monika exclaimed. "If you're sure I'd fit in."

"Come here at seven tomorrow evening. I'll take you. Just remember not to mention it to anyone—even your aunt and uncle."

"I won't," Monika promised. "I'll see you tomorrow night."

Manfred stood in the doorway, watching her as she walked away. She took a breath as she rounded the corner. The meeting the following evening would reveal how deep this network went.

7

The meeting was in a basement a mile from Manfred's house. A man with a twirling mustache that failed to cover pock marks on his cheeks led them through the storm door in the back of his house. He introduced himself as Egon and introduced them to two other men, Claus, a small man with blond hair, and Anton, who was in his early 50s. There were no flags adorning the walls or pictures of Hitler staring down, but the men's rhetoric made it very clear where their loyalties lay. They sat in a circle in the clean space of the small, unfinished basement. Pipes creaked as Egon cleared his throat. He went over much of the same ground as Manfred had the night before, and Monika told her cover story about her non-existent alcoholic father.

After she'd finished, Egon began again. "Our mission is to improve the lives of loyal German citizens. If we let other countries walk all over us as we did after the Great War, we'll never return to our rightful place among the world's great nations again."

Anton asked him a question. "Is it possible we can take on the might of the United States and win?"

Egon grinned as he replied. "Absolutely. Hitler showed what he was capable of in 1940. We took more territory in a week than the Kaiser did during the last war in four years. With the Führer to guide us, we're capable of anything."

"Are we preparing for an invasion? Can we take mainland America?" Monika asked to prove that she was one of them. None of the other men questioned her.

"We won't need to. The American public will soon grow tired of the foreign war their president has dragged them into, and the troops will return. Once they do, Europe will be ours, and Hitler's dream for the German people will come true," Manfred said.

Monika nodded at Manfred, hoping he believed she could accept this warped version of reality.

"But who among us is prepared to do more than just talk?" Manfred demanded. "We come to this basement, week in and week out, and discuss the merits of Hitler's plans versus the twisted system in place in this country, but that's all we do."

"What do you want from us?" Egon asked incredulously. "To storm the White House?"

The others laughed.

Manfred shook his head in frustration. Monika looked on from her seat.

The rest of the meeting continued in the same vein. By the time Monika left, it was apparent that this wasn't the dangerous underground cell that she was seeking. But perhaps Manfred himself knew more.

It was close to eleven o'clock when they left. Manfred seemed frustrated. "Talk, talk, talk, that's all those fools are prepared to do. We can't represent the Führer by debating the benefits of his policies in a basement."

"I know, it's ridiculous, but those men have lives here. Jobs and families. They're loyal to Germany but don't want to upset what they've built here."

Manfred whirled around to face her. "What about you?"

"Me?"

"What are you prepared to do to make Germany the greatest nation in the world?" he spat.

Her words were resolute.

"I am prepared to do more. I just don't know that I'd be willing to kill anyone."

They stopped talking for a few seconds as they passed a man walking his dog and began again.

"You might find you have a different outlook one day. No one wants to kill for their country. No one in their right mind, anyway. But sometimes, we're forced to reach beyond what we're comfortable with and sacrifice our own moral outlook in service of the cause."

"But suppose by fighting here in America we make things worse for Germany."

Manfred frowned. "You seriously believe that Roosevelt, Churchill and that savage, Stalin, have anything but the annihilation of Germany in mind? It's time to wake up, Greta. The future of the Fatherland is at stake. There's no telling what the Bolshevist hordes will do if they ever get onto German soil. They would rape, pillage and destroy everyone and everything in their path. Make no mistake, this war presents an existential moment in time for the German people. What's your conscience going to whisper to you in the middle of the night if you don't do all you can to prevent the destruction of the German nation?"

She hesitated.

Manfred pushed his point. "And even if you don't agree with some of the Nazis' policies," he said. "Is it worth the annihilation of the German people?"

Monika didn't want to seem too eager, so she played coy again. "I can see your point, but I need some time to think it over."

They walked in silence for a few seconds. The block of houses ended, and they passed some waste ground overlooking the bay.

A car appeared out of nowhere, drove past, and then screeched to a halt across the pavement in front of them.

Two men in suits got out of the car holding pistols. "Don't think about doing anything stupid," a tall man with black hair said in a German accent.

"What's the meaning of this?" Manfred said.

Monika turned to him. "You don't know these men?"

"Come with me, Manfred," one of the men said, gesturing toward the wasteland leading down to the water.

Manfred walked away with his hands up. The other man went behind him. "What are you going to do?" she heard Manfred say.

"You've betrayed the Fatherland by bringing a spy to your ridiculous meeting," the man with the pistol responded.

Shock struck Monika like a bucket of cold water in the face.

The other man had his gun trained on her. "Move and you die," he growled. "Hands behind your back." He put handcuffs on her and then took a black hood from his pocket and slipped it over her head.

Monika stood motionless, unable to see through the opaque material of the hood. In the background, she heard a brief struggle and Manfred pleading for his life. Then, a gunshot and silence. Her blood turned to ice.

"It's done," one of her assailants said. "Get her in the car."

"What did you do to him?" she said.

Her answer was a slap in the face. "Keep your mouth shut if you want to live through this."

Rough hands grabbed her. Monika tried to shake them off but felt the barrel of a pistol pressed into her back.

"We can end this all right here and now," the voice said. "Or you can get into the trunk."

They put her in the trunk of the car and shut it. The little light she could see through the material of the hood was extinguished, and the world went black.

She told herself to stay calm and not panic. Manfred's death meant there was one less Nazi in the world. *Stay focused, Monika.*

Monika tried to track how long she was in the trunk and the turns the car made, but it was impossible in an area she didn't know. Her best guess was that she was in there for around 20 minutes, but that was all she could account for. She remembered her training and the hours of counter-interrogation measures she'd been taught, but even her instructors had admitted that they were little more than delaying tactics. Everyone broke in the end. The measure of a recruit was how long they took.

The trunk opened, and fresh air came flooding into the enclosed space. She heard the same voices and felt hands on her once more. All pretense was now gone. The men were speaking German between themselves. It seemed she'd found the underground cell.

"Get her inside," one said.

Her instinct was to fight them at every turn, but she figured her best chance to get out of this was to see what they wanted and to play the dumb, innocent, confused German girl at every turn. Monika walked with them.

She knew full well she'd receive no answer but asked the questions anyway. "Where am I? What do you want with me?"

She tried to make out the details of where they were taking her through the minuscule slits in the hood over her head, but it wasn't possible to garner anything useful. She tried to focus on what she knew—A car had pulled up, and two men had gotten out. She'd heard them speaking German.

They threw her into a wooden chair with her hands behind her, then tied her ankles to the legs of the chair.

"Are you going to talk to me now?" she said in English. "What's this all about?"

One of the men dragged the hood off the top of her head. "Let's speak in our native tongue," he said in German. "We'll be more comfortable that way."

Monika looked around. She was in a small, sparsely decorated house. Two lamps shone in her face; there were no other lights. The drapes were closed. She was in the living room. The man who'd spoken was in his early 30s, with short black hair and stubble to match. No one had masks on, which worried her.

"All right," Monika said in German. "What am I doing here?"

The other man stepped forward with a canteen in his hand. He offered it to her. "You must be thirsty." He was around the same age as the first but smaller. He had blue eyes and short blond hair. The blond man held the canteen to her lips, and she drank.

"I need to use the bathroom," she said.

The first man laughed. "There'll be time for that."

"What did you do to my friend?"

"Don't worry about him. The police will find his body soon enough." He got down on his haunches to face her. "The real question is, are you going to join him in death?"

"What do you want from me?"

"We know what you were doing at the meeting tonight."

"I don't know what you're talking about. Who are you?"

The man smiled. "You can call me Otto. Why have you chosen to join up with the enemies of the Fatherland?"

"Why did you do that? Why did you shoot poor Manfred? He was loyal to the Führer!"

Otto shook his head. "Details. Just details. Let's talk about more important things, like why you've decided to betray your country."

"I'm a patriotic German," Monika answered. "Loyal to the German people."

Otto slapped her across the face in full force.

"Why did you train to fight for a country that doesn't care about you? Why would you betray your country and offer your services to a foreign power that wants to destroy the Fatherland and everything we hold dear?" Her head rocked back as the sting spread across her cheek. Her vision dimmed, and she heard a ringing in her ears. "Make no mistake. We're in charge here. Think of your friend and realize the situation you're in."

"You've got the wrong person," she grunted.

Monika was ready for the slap this time, but it still hurt just as much.

"Tell us your real name."

"Greta Manninger is my real name."

"Your name is Monika Ritter. We know everything about you, so stop lying," Otto snarled. "You're only alive because you're useful to us."

"I'm just an ordinary—"

"Tell us everything you know about your dirty network of spies. What they're doing, where they're going...."

"I don't know what you're talking about. You're wasting your time."

"You know exactly what I'm talking about. Where are you from?"

If they knew her name, there was no point in lying about this. "Berlin."

Otto nodded. "Good. Now we're getting to the truth. Monika Ritter from Berlin."

"What are you talking about? Just let me go. Let me go!"

Otto was calm in his demeanor. "You're a smart girl, Monika. You wouldn't be here if you weren't. We're not going to let you go until we find out everything you know. And if we don't, we're not going to let you go. You already know how serious we are."

She struggled against the ropes but only succeeded in shifting the chair a few inches.

"What do you want?"

"We want what you possess."

"And what might that be?"

He patted her on the shoulder with a smile. "Information, Monika. How about we start with your new assignment in Switzerland?"

How do they know about that?

"I don't know what you're talking about."

"We'll keep you here as long as we need to. What happens next is up to you, Monika. The road map is in your hands. We're just here to facilitate whatever occurs."

All I have to do is betray everything I hold most dear, she thought to herself. *After which, they'll kill me anyway.*

"I'll leave you to think about it with Hans for a while." Otto walked out of the living room.

Hans, the other man, almost seemed nervous. "Would you like some water?" he said after a few minutes.

Monika nodded, and the German agent went to fetch a canteen. He held it to her lips, and she drank. He returned to the couch, sat down, lit a cigarette, and picked up an Agatha Christie novel. It was in English.

As time went on, Monika began to tire. Even with her hands manacled behind her back, her eyelids became heavier. The next thing she knew, Hans was tapping her on the cheek. She opened her eyes. They felt like they were full of sand.

"No time for sleep, Monika."

∼

Everything ached: her back, her legs, her wrists, and her arms. Whenever she tried to rest her eyes, Hans was in her face to wake her up, either by slapping her on the cheek or throwing water. Morning came, but Monika hadn't slept. Exhaustion overtook her body, infecting her like a virus and clouding her mind. She knew the actual interrogation had yet to begin, and she was terrified she would break and reveal details about her fellow spies that could endanger their lives.

The interrogation began again in the afternoon. The two Germans covered the same ground as the night before. Monika said little. They gave her some bread and water for lunch and dinner and resumed as the daylight faded to black.

It must have been after midnight when Otto stopped questioning her. He stood up from the chair as his colleague walked over.

"No sleep for her tonight. She'll break tomorrow."

He left the room and went upstairs. Hans settled into his familiar position of sitting on the couch with a paperback in his hand.

What could she do to escape? If she tried and failed, she would end up like Manfred, dead on the waste ground with a bullet in the back of her head.

Thinking was hard. Her brain was listless and slow. She longed for the sleep that would cure all her ills but knew these men wouldn't grant it to her until they deemed she had earned it.

She wriggled and groaned in the chair.

"I need to use the bathroom."

Hans put the book down and walked over. He untied her legs, leaving her hands shackled behind her back. She stretched out as she stood. It felt good, but her arms still ached. He took a pistol from his pocket.

"Follow me," he said. He jabbed the end of the gun into her back as he marched her through the house.

The front door was next to the living room. Monika tried to peer through the translucent black glass but saw nothing. She passed through a small kitchen. It didn't look lived in.

"Open the door," Hans said. "And don't try anything."

She did as the man said and walked out into an open backyard with nothing on either side. There were no neighbors, and the only light was from the stars, which dotted the sky above like diamonds spread on black velvet. They were in the countryside, with nothing to signify exactly where. The outhouse was twenty feet behind the main house.

"You've got one minute," he said.

"Can you at least uncuff me?"

"You'll manage."

"I can't use the toilet if I can't pull my pants down, can I?"

Hans shook his head and reached into his pocket. He unlocked her handcuffs. The relief was instantaneous. She rubbed her wrists as if bringing them back to life.

She thought to take him out with a chop to the side of his throat, but he was already standing back, pointing his gun at her.

He motioned for her to hurry up, and she closed the outhouse door behind her. A thousand thoughts ran through her mind, but they all coalesced as one notion—how she could escape. She steeled herself for what was about to come, taking a moment in the dark alone to gather her thoughts into some kind of workable plan. There was nothing around here—no one to run to. She'd have to find someone fast.

The outhouse was freezing cold. Monika peered through a tiny gap in the wood and saw Hans standing three feet from the door with the gun in his hand.

She might not get a better chance.

"Come on, Monika. Don't dawdle. Get out of there."

"What?" she replied.

She pressed her eye to the tiny gap in the wood. He seemed annoyed.

"Get out of there before I come in and drag you out," he said.

Monika unlocked the door as quietly as she could and looked through at the man again.

"Come on!"

It was time. "I can't get out," she mumbled. She pulled on the lock, holding the door shut. "I think there's something caught in the lock. Can you take a look from your side?"

Hans grumbled to himself for a second but agreed. She watched him come within a few inches of the door, moved back onto the toilet seat, and then kicked as hard as she could with both feet. The solid wood crashed into Hans's head, and he hurtled backward. She jumped out and made for the pistol. It was on the grass a few inches from his hand. Monika got to it first and struck him in the head with the barrel, not wanting to attract attention by firing it. His body went still.

Not knowing which direction to run, she headed toward a clump of woods about 300 yards away. She was halfway there when she heard shouting from behind her. Hans was on his feet and roaring after her. Monika knew she was in a race now. The only way to win was to make it back to civilization first. There were no houses or even roads nearby. Not that she could see in the darkness, anyway.

Monika looked back as she entered the woods. Hans was 200 yards behind her now. Otto was 100 yards behind him. She bolted through the trees, knowing that she was dead if the Nazi agents caught her. The only sensible thing to do with her now was to kill her—the same as they'd done to Manfred, who was one of their own. They wouldn't hesitate now and would likely shoot on sight. The stakes were clear.

Most of the light disappeared in the thick of the woods. She had to slow down, feeling her way along. The ground was clear, but she still used the trees to navigate, going from one to the next. The German agents were behind her. She could hear their voices as they entered the forest. She kept going. Being here was dangerous, but she doubted she could beat two men in a foot race after two days of being tied to a chair. Her limbs were sluggish and sore. No matter how she tried to push her body, it wouldn't respond. It was all she could do to keep moving forward. She longed to rest, even for a few seconds, but she resisted the voices inside telling her to stop and kept going. A low-hanging tree branch seemed to come out of nowhere, and she fell to the soft ground. Blood started dripping from her mouth. She moved her hand to stifle the flow before standing up once more. Dizzier now, she put a hand on the tree that had taken her out and looked back to see where her captors were. She heard them calling out to each other. They were closer now—perhaps only 50 yards behind her. A gunshot sounded. Were they shooting at her or trying to find each other? Her legs burned. Breath thundered in and out of her lungs.

She thought of Manfred. The police would have found him by now. Perhaps Albarn and Shipley were out looking for her.

The trees ended as suddenly as they'd begun, and Monika found herself on a long road. It must have been after midnight, but after a few seconds of hiding, she saw the bright lights of a vehicle approaching. The thought that this might have been another German agent who wasn't chasing her through the woods occurred to her, but she had to risk it.

Monika stood in the middle of the road waving her arms as the pickup truck slowed down. A man stuck his head out of the window. He seemed drunk.

"What are you doing all the way out here, girlie?"

She ran to the driver's side door as Hans and Otto emerged from the forest about 200 yards from where the truck had stopped and flagged down another passing car.

"I need your truck," Monika said urgently.

"Now, wait just a minute…"

Monika dragged him out and got into the driver's seat. The man held drunkenly onto the door.

"What d'you think you're doing?"

A shot rang out. The driver turned around to see where the noise had come from, and Monika stepped on the gas. The man spun around and fell on the road, then scrambled to his feet and staggered after her.

"Hey, get back here!"

She checked the rearview mirror and saw that the German agents had also procured a passing car. They were coming after her. They sped past the owner of the truck, almost hitting him.

Monika was about 300 yards ahead of the car, but it was gaining. She pushed her foot all the way down, but the truck was old and slow and was struggling to respond. The car was a hundred yards back now, and she saw Hans leaning out the passenger side window to point a gun. She swerved as he fired, and the shot missed. She steered the vehicle from one side of the deserted road to the other but lost speed in doing so. The car was almost on her rear bumper. Hans shot again. He was aiming at the tires, trying to slow her down rather than kill her. Perhaps that would come later.

Monika hit the brake and let Otto come up beside her, then rammed into the car with the heavier pickup truck. The vehicle veered off to the side of the road, and she accelerated on, looking for a town, a police car, or someone to scare the Germans off. The road was pitch-black, but up ahead, the glow of streetlights cut through the darkness. The sign for a town flashed past. The car was still just a few yards behind, but the man wasn't shooting now. Monika scanned the empty shopfronts for somewhere to take refuge. Everything was closed. If she got out on an empty street, the men would scoop her up and bring her back to the house to finish her off. She had no idea where she was or where the next town might be.

She drove past the main street, increasingly desperate, with the German agents right behind her. She was about to give up when she saw a coffee shop on the edge of town with a police car outside. The lights were still on, and she pulled over, almost crashing into the parked patrol car. The vehicle with the Germans pulled up on the street. She jumped out and ran inside. The policeman, who looked about 25, was sitting at the counter with a cup in his hand. He stood up as she ran toward him.

"There's someone following me," she said in her best American English.

The policeman stood up.

"They're outside," she said between breaths. "Two men were chasing me!"

The cop ran outside, but the street was dead.

"I'm not from here," Monika said. "Can I sleep in the police station tonight until someone comes for me tomorrow morning?"

The policeman looked at her as if she was insane.

The same policeman who'd brought her in the night before woke Monika the next morning. The door to the cell she'd slept in was open, and she walked out to the reception area, where one of her instructors, whom she only knew to see, was waiting for her. He held out a hand to her. "My name's Brinkley. You know who I am, don't you?"

"Sergeant Dover called you, I assume." The young policeman was standing watching them. "Thanks," she said.

"Let's get you back to camp and cleaned up," Brinkley said. "You'll be fully briefed when we arrive back at Catoctin. In the meantime, don't ask questions I'm not cleared to answer."

Now that she was finally safe, the full weight of what she'd been through brought itself to bear on her. She stared out the window in silence for the duration of the 30-minute ride back to the camp. Driving through the gates felt like coming home.

"Come with me, "Brinkley said. "You can clean yourself off after your debrief."

He led her to a new prefabricated building used as a meeting room and held the door open for her. Albarn and Shipley were sitting with Bill Hayden.

"I didn't expect to see you here, sir," Monika told Hayden.

"That's the least of your surprises," he replied with a knowing grin.

"Come in, gentlemen!" Albarn shouted toward a door at the back of the room. Otto, Manfred, and Hans walked through.

"What?" Monika exclaimed.

"This is Otto Schmidt, Manfred Manteuffel and Hans Lipbarski. All are OSS recruits in training like you. We had to see what you were made of. Mr. Dulles insisted on it," Albarn said. "He wants to take you on, Ritter. But it was my idea to do this. We have something special planned for you."

"Sorry, Ritter," Otto said in German.

"This was another training exercise?" Monika gasped. "Why?"

"We have to be sure our German recruits can resist being turned," Hayden said.

"Did I pass?" she asked.

"With flying colors," Albarn replied.

"What if those bullets had hit me, or my tire had burst, and I flipped over when you were chasing me?" she said to Otto.

"We really didn't want you to escape. Our assignment was to try to turn you," Otto responded. "And then, you got away!"

"In other words, you failed in your mission," Shipley snarled at Otto, clearly pleased to have someone to criticize.

"I think anyone would have failed when it comes to trying to get the better of Monika," Albarn said, winking at Otto.

"You're not wrong," Hayden added.

"How's your head, Hans?" Monika asked.

The German recruit pointed at a bruise in the middle of his forehead where the outhouse door had hit him. "You got me a good one, but I'll survive."

"Well done," Albarn said and patted her on the shoulder. "Outstanding work."

She felt a surge of pride. Praise from him seemed worth more than from anyone else.

Shipley looked at the ground by his feet and remained quiet.

"All right, go get cleaned up, Ritter. You have another debrief in here at 1100 hours," Albarn said.

Monika walked out into the sunlight. A smile spread across her face. A squad of new recruits jogged past. She knew she was no longer one of them. Her time here was almost at an end.

8

Monika took all the time she could in the shower, luxuriating in the feeling of the warm water on her skin. Her body still ached from the ordeal the OSS agents had put her through. Her wrists were raw where the handcuffs had touched her skin, and her ankles ached from the ropes that had held her in place. It seemed Dulles wanted her on his team. She had been dreaming of a posting to Switzerland every day during training but had never dared say it out loud. Now, her wish was to be granted.

She turned off the water and toweled herself down, taking extra care of her wrists and ankles. The barracks was empty as she dressed. All the other recruits were out running or trying to negotiate the obstacle course as the instructors screamed at them. Not being out among them was a great relief. The change in her body and mind had been evident during her captivity. No way would she have been able to withstand that experience before her training. She was more physically resilient than she'd ever been, but more than that, her will was sturdier than the Brooklyn Bridge now. She was proud of how she'd held up but knew that her experience was nothing in comparison to how the Gestapo would have treated her.

The clean clothes she changed into felt heavenly. There was no mirror in the barracks, but she was confident in how she must have looked. She walked out to the meeting room and sat down five minutes before it was scheduled to begin.

Albarn and Hayden walked in two minutes later with Otto.

"I can't shake you Otto, can I?"

"I'm part of the deal," he answered.

Albarn had a manila folder under his arm. He placed it on the table and began to speak.

"Your recent experience was part of a warmup assignment for Otto and his friends. But more importantly, it was a test of your mettle. And thankfully for us all, you were up to the task. Now, we need you to use the skills you've learned in the field, but this time I can guarantee it won't be a training exercise."

Albarn drew two large photographs from his folder. He handed one to Monika and the other to Otto. The pictures were of two separate ships. One was half-sunk, propped up by ropes and scaffolding, and the other was almost fully submerged.

"These photos are from the harbor in Baltimore last week. Two destroyers were sabotaged. It was a sophisticated operation. Most likely frogmen who came in at night. It's hard to tell, but we think they planted limpet mines before escaping. Thankfully no sailors were hurt in either of the blasts, but the saboteurs caused millions of dollars of damage. The boys down at the port don't know whether they can salvage that one or not." He pointed to the photo in Monika's hands.

"Was anyone caught?" Monika asked.

"No," Hayden said. "They came in, planted the bombs, and disappeared into the night."

"It seems likely we're dealing with an underground cell," Albarn said.

"German agents in our midst," Hayden added. "For real this time."

"Did the police find out anything?" she asked.

"No. That could mean that the cell isn't based in this area, or else it might just be that they're meticulous and careful. Either way, their mission at the docks was a massive success for them."

"Were any other bombs found?" Otto asked.

"No," Hayden replied. "No wastage. The entire site was swept. Nothing else was found."

"So, they were highly trained and organized. It seems like a matter of time before they strike again," Monika said.

"Now's about the time I'm sure you're beginning to wonder what you're doing here," Albarn said. "There was a break-in at the docks in New York a week before the attack on Baltimore. Some blueprints and some schedules were taken. No one was caught, but the police found a fingerprint on one of the desks. It was from this man."

Albarn returned to the folder and handed Monika a photograph of a balding man in his early 40s.

"His name is Werner Kerling. He spent 18 months behind bars in New York in the early 30s for breaking and entering, but as far as we know, he's been clean ever since. We don't know a lot about him other than that he left the country in '36 and came back just before the war kicked off in '39. He's been living in Orlando, Florida, ever since.

"Is he a U.S. citizen?" Otto asked.

"Yes, he is," Albarn answered. "We're certain Kerling isn't acting alone. We don't know the identities of the other men he's working with or even how many of them there might be."

"Why him?"

"His name came from an informant," Hayden answered.

"If you have an informant, why do you need me?"

"The snitch led us to him but didn't seem to know much

else," Hayden stated before continuing. "We don't know a thing about the others or what they're planning next, but that's where you come in," Hayden said. "Agents of the FBI have been watching Herr Kerling for a couple of weeks now. At first, they followed him to his job on a construction site and thought nothing of it. But about a week ago, they heard him send a radio signal."

"How?" Otto asked.

"A listening device in his house. It transmits back a signal to them," Hayden continued. "He contacted another German spy who told him they were sending a special agent in the next few weeks. This agent was to organize them even further and had a special mission she'd debrief them about."

"She?" Monika asked.

"Yes. Greta is her name." Albarn said. "The instructions Kerling received were to meet the agent on a beach in North Florida and bring her ashore. He was to get back to them with a date and time." He turned to Monika. "We want you to stand in for that agent and bring the rest of the cell to us."

Monika nodded, hoping the nerves inside her weren't showing on her face. "But when the real Nazi shows up—"

"She won't. Our men broke into the house the day after we sent Kerling the message. They messaged Germany an arrival point for the agent, met her, and arrested her. She is being held captive and debriefed as we speak. Then the FBI procured the wavelength the message was sent on, and then we sent our own to Kerling, with directions to pick you up at a specific date and time. So, the only agent he'll meet is you, Ritter."

"Where do I come in?" Otto asked.

"Monika will come in on a sub. She's going to need a German sailor to help her row ashore. You've received theoretical training in marine landings. We'll take you out before the operation to show you how to land in practice. We don't want you getting washed up on shore. It wouldn't look good."

Monika understood the physical element of the plan but needed to figure out what was to follow. "So, Otto helps me row into shore. Then what?"

"Then he goes back to the submarine and returns to port," Albarn said. "It will be your job to infiltrate the German spy ring. Get as much info as you can on their plans. Then, we'll swoop in and pick them up."

It all sounded so simple. Perhaps it would be, but in Monika's experience, few things ever worked out that way. "When do we move out?" she asked.

"Today is Tuesday. The arrangement is to meet at 0300 hours on Saturday morning," Albarn said. "Take some time to relax. You've been through a lot the last couple of nights."

"Who will I be? What's my persona?"

"Your code name is Greta. Apart from that, to the best of our knowledge, the central command didn't share much information about who they were sending," Albarn said. "You're from Berlin, so if anyone asks, you'd be best advised to say that's where you're from, but I don't think you'll be sitting down with Kerling and whoever else and chatting into the wee hours. As far as the fake operation you're going to set up —you'll be assigned a handler in Florida. If you have to leave the area, you'll be given a phone number to call. We're not going to leave you high and dry, Ritter. You can be assured of that."

"Weapons?"

"You'll be issued a standard German Walther PP38 to land with," Albarn said.

"And one of those knives you invented?" she replied.

Albarn nodded with a smile.

"What about papers, plans, money to organize the troops?"

"We're working on fake IDs for you and a social security card too. They'll all be ready by the time you leave. You'll also be issued with $25,000. The men will expect you to fund their missions. It wouldn't do to have you show up with a pocketful of pennies," Albarn said.

Otto patted Monika on the shoulder. "You're rich, Ritter! You made it!"

"The money must be accounted for," Hayden said. "And you'll be expected to return whatever you don't spend."

"Those Nazi insurgents always eat in the best restaurants, don't they? And only stay in five-star hotels!" Otto added with a smile.

After a few days recovering at the camp in Catoctin, Monika packed up her bags and left the barracks she'd lived in for the previous three months. The air was cold as she stepped outside. She was glad not to be training here as the weather changed. It was hard enough in the warmth of autumn, but it might have been unbearable in the cold of winter. She could only imagine crawling through freezing cold mud as the instructors shot live rounds over the recruits' heads. She was destined for warmer climes, thankful the Germans had decided to land in Florida, not Maine.

Monika took the last 15 minutes in the camp to walk around alone. She wouldn't miss being here but wanted to pay homage to the place. Otto was waiting by their barracks. She had spoken to him a little the previous day. It would have been an exaggeration to say they'd formed a friendship, but she knew him somewhat now. He was amusing and intelligent. He was being posted to London in a few weeks.

A truck pulled up, and Brinkley, the man who'd driven her back from the police station two nights before, jumped out.

Albarn and Shipley walked up a few seconds later. Shipley shook her hand—no words of contrition or congratulations, just a handshake. He handed her a backpack with her IDs and other fake papers inside. "The money's in a pouch at the front," he said. Look after it."

Monika took the backpack and checked the front pouch. Two wads of $100 bills sat there. She picked one up and examined it. She had never seen so much money in her life, let alone held it.

"Ritter, I have something for you," Albarn said. He reached into his pocket and handed her one of the slim fighting knives he'd designed. "It's a good one. It won't let you down. Remember—no mercy in the field. It's kill or be killed."

Monika took the knife and held it up. "Thank you. I won't let you down."

"Good luck," the Englishman said.

She climbed into the truck and left Camp Catoctin for the last time.

She and Otto arrived at Norfolk Naval Base in Virginia as the afternoon faded. Brinkley dropped them off at the central administrative building, where a young officer who introduced himself as Ward greeted them with enthusiastic handshakes and led them into a debriefing room.

"We leave port on Thursday morning and sail down to the meeting point." He picked up the piece of paper on the desk in front of him. "I believe it's set at Crescent Beach, just north of the small town of Marineland on Florida's Atlantic Coast. It's lovely down there. Have you ever been?"

"I haven't had the pleasure," Monika replied with a smile.

"A lovely lady like you will fit right in."

Monika ignored the comment. She stayed quiet as the young naval officer led them through the bustling base to the submarine docks.

"Have you done a night landing before?"

"Not from a submarine," Otto replied. "But I assume it's the same as from a regular boat."

"It can be a little tricky, but we'll take you offshore to practice tonight. I'm sure you'll be just fine after that."

"Will the contact notice the difference between the German and American submarines?" Monika asked. "I'm concerned that he might watch us disembark through a pair of binoculars."

"I don't know what kind of a submarine expert this man you're meeting will be, but our boat will raise the Nazi flag to reassure him. I don't anticipate any problems there."

Ward walked them onto the dock and showed them the submarine they would take out that night and down to Florida.

"It doesn't seem right raising the Nazi flag on the old girl," he said with a shake of his head. He led them back to the mess hall, where dinner was being served. Monika looked around at the sea of sailors in the massive hall as she ate. She was the only woman not serving food.

The weather helped. The clouds overhead covered the stars and the moon's rays, adding an extra layer of darkness to the night. Monika was dressed in black. Otto wore a German sailor's outfit. He'd be shot as a spy if he was caught in civilian clothes. If Monika had been a real spy, she would have had to take her chances. The interior of the submarine was cramped and sweaty. Otto pulled at the tight collar of his shirt. He had put on a coat over it to hide that it was at least two sizes too small for him.

Monika didn't enjoy being stuck inside and was glad when the vice-captain came to tell them they were on the surface. The coast of Florida was in sight. The vice-captain, a handsome young sailor named Clegg, invited Monika to look through the periscope. She saw a dark length of ocean, which led to an even darker blob at the horizon.

"That's the beach," Clegg said. "That's where you're meeting the target."

As the sub came to a halt, a sailor opened the hatch. Otto and Monika carried up the raft and inflated it. Another sailor held the raft steady as they got in.

"Only in German from this point," Monika announced as they set off from the submarine. Her colleague took the left oar of the yellow dinghy. It was several hundred yards to shore. It was difficult to tell exactly how far in the darkness. Thankfully, the ocean was calm, and they made swift progress through the small waves. As they drew closer, Monika scanned the coastline for the contact. They were about a hundred yards out when she saw an outline of what looked like a person standing on the beach.

"Steer to port. I think I see him."

They lowered their oars once more. Monika took deep breaths in through her nose as they neared the beach. This man would kill her if he suspected anything. If he and the other conspirators were American citizens, they faced the death sentence for treason against the Republic.

A light appeared as they came within 50 yards of the shore. He was directing them in with a flashlight.

"Follow the flashlight," Monika said.

"Do you forgive me for tying you to that chair?" Otto whispered.

"I thank you for it," Monika answered.

They jumped out and dragged the dinghy ashore, up to their ankles. Monika turned as the contact approached. She recognized him from the photo Albarn had shown her at Catoctin, although he was slightly balder now.

"Heil Hitler," she said to him.

"Heil Hitler."

She shook his hand. "Good to meet you. You can call me Greta."

"Werner Kerling."

"This is Otto. He'll leave us now."

"Good luck, Greta," Otto said as he launched the dingy back into the ocean and rowed away. Monika was alone.

"Anyone else with you?" she asked as the contact led her off the beach.

"No. We'll meet them tomorrow."

"You have a car?"

"Just over the dunes."

They walked across the deserted beach in silence. Monika scanned up and down, but there was no one else. The nearest town's population was measured in dozens and had only been founded two years before. The Abwehr, the German intelligence force, had chosen a good place to land their operative.

"You tired?" Kerling said to her as they walked between two dunes.

"I'm okay. I got some sleep on the boat."

A 1932 Ford Model T was parked by the side of a dirt track. Monika noted the license plate before climbing in.

"Where are we going?" she asked.

"A motel a few miles away." His hands were shaking on the steering wheel.

"Did you get the last signal we sent through?" Monika asked.

Kerling shook his head as he pulled onto the road. "Some bum broke into my apartment and ransacked the place. They took the radio and a few other things."

"You won't need that now, anyway. I'll take care of all communications with the Abwehr. When did you receive your training?"

"I went back in '36. I wanted to experience life under the National Socialists. It was glorious, but my brother-in-law suggested I could serve the Reich better by coming back here. I joined the Abwehr in '38 and moved to Orlando in '39."

"Why there?"

"It's a pretty nondescript place, and everyone there's a migrant of some kind. I do casual work and come and go as I please. No one asks too many questions. I can keep an eye on the Army Air Base. Those flyers like to drink, and when they do, they start talking."

She wanted to ask what he'd done in service of the Reich to that point but held herself back. Patience was going to be key here.

"I want to meet the other men as soon as possible. Where do they live?"

"In Philadelphia and Delaware."

"Do they know I'm here?"

"I told two of them. The third is new. I'm not 100% on him yet."

"Good. I'll research and decide overnight where we are going to meet and leave the rest to you."

"What do you have for us?"

"Too much to go into right now, but I can guarantee you that we're going to step up our operations from here. I met with Admiral Canaris personally last week. He's expecting big things. We went through a list of targets."

Kerling agreed but didn't ask any more questions.

They drove along the bumpy dirt track in silence. Monika saw nothing. No lights or people until the track ended.

They arrived at a small, rundown motel on the side of the highway that led into the city. Kerling handed her a key as they arrived. "I'm in room 218," he said.

"I'll find you in the morning and give you your orders," she answered.

Monika got out of the car and went to her room. She shut the door behind her, wary of slipping back into her own personality. She afforded herself a moment's thought for Michael before spiraling into a deep sleep.

She and Kerling had breakfast in a local diner half a mile down the road, full of truckers who looked at her as if she were the first woman they'd ever seen. She was glad that none spoke to her, and she used her best American accent when ordering her eggs after instructing Kerling to say nothing. Extra attention was the last thing she needed here.

After they'd eaten, she handed him a napkin with the name of the Warwick Hotel written on it. It was a place one of the other recruits at Catoctin had mentioned before and seemed as good a meeting place as any other.

"You and your men will meet me in the lobby of this hotel in Philadelphia at 3 PM next Tuesday afternoon."

"What shall I tell them?"

"Tell them to come ready to work. I'll see you in a few days up north."

She returned to her room and gathered the few belongings she'd brought from the submarine. The enormous amount of the government's money she carried weighed heavily as she walked out. Her mind turned to Michael. He was still in training in Georgia. She couldn't even write to him now. She walked into the city and found the bus station.

Two hours later, the bus to Washington, DC, pulled out of the station. It was time to check in with her handler—Bill Hayden.

9

Monika checked into the hotel Hayden had told her to use in central DC. She resisted the temptation to call Michael's family in New York, choosing to live out her days as Greta instead. It was best for her that way. It was too dangerous to go back and forth between her real life and the false one she was presenting to the Abwehr agents. After spending the night in a good hotel alone, she went to the Washington Monument. It took her a few minutes to find the mailbox, but when she did, Monika took some chalk she'd brought and marked it with three straight lines. Making sure no one had seen her, she dropped the chalk back in her pocket and walked away. She had some time to waste and strolled up the mall toward the Lincoln Memorial. This wasn't a city she knew. She and Michael had talked about visiting but had never gotten around to it. The only previous time she'd come was to harass Hayden into letting her join the OSS. The mall was a wave of activity, with construction going on all over and hundreds of people crisscrossing it. Soldiers and sailors passed her. Men in suits and women pushing strollers. It felt good to be a part of this. Her life had brought her here. It was truly amazing. In '36, she'd been convinced that her story was over. She had been prepared to die if it meant getting even for her father's death at the hands of the Nazis. Michael had been the one to foil her plan to get close enough to Goebbels to assassinate him. Michael saved her life.

It was a fine, crisp morning, and she kept on all the way down to the Lincoln Memorial. It was breathtaking. She stood among a group of schoolchildren and gazed up at the giant statue of the man they called the Great Emancipator. She wondered why she'd been so determined to join the OSS and risk her life for a country she'd never been to before. Her parents appeared in her mind. She could almost hear their voices. It was as if they were standing beside her, marveling at the magnificent statue and all it represented. She felt their pride in her. That was enough. She turned around to gaze back along the reflecting pool and wondered if she'd ever return to live in Germany.

"Not until the Nazi curse is eradicated," she said under her breath.

She wandered among the schoolchildren and the tourists for several more hours, acting as if she hadn't a care in the world for just one afternoon.

The illusion of freedom was shattered as she returned to the hotel. Hayden was in the lobby reading a newspaper. The OSS man put it down as she walked over. She sat down opposite him and said, "Room 310."

Hayden followed her up five minutes later. He walked through the door without greeting her and took a seat at a small round table by the window. He reached into a leather briefcase he'd brought and took out a bottle of whiskey and a manila folder.

"Drink?" he said.

Whiskey wasn't Monika's favorite, but she agreed. She took two glasses from the sideboard and sat opposite him.

"Did the landing go well?" he began after he'd poured the drinks.

Monika recounted every detail of the landing and what had happened afterward.

"So, you're meeting the rest of the crew in the Warwick Hotel in central Philadelphia on Tuesday?" Hayden said. "Do you know anything about them yet?"

"Kerling was sparse with the details."

"The important part is to uncover any plans they already have in motion."

"That could take time, even if they are convinced that I am who I say I am."

"If you take charge, they'll open up. but don't underestimate how dangerous these men are. They haven't killed yet that we know of, but it's only a matter of time. Try to feel them out. See who the brains of the operation is."

Hayden finished his glass of whiskey and poured himself another. "I used to do this exact same thing with your father-in-law in Berlin," he said.

"Drink with him in hotel rooms?"

"While engaging in sensitive discussions."

"He never said."

"Then he understood the nature of our meetings. Have you decided how you're going to proceed?"

"As we discussed, I'm going to find out the power structure of the group I meet in Philly. See who their natural leader is and get his confidence."

Hayden rolled the amber liquid around his glass. "He might have problems with the fact you're a woman. Nazi sympathizers won't be the most forward-thinking people you'll ever meet."

"Nothing I haven't been dealing with my whole life." She took a sip of whiskey and picked up the list again. A surge of nervous energy flooded her veins, but she used the breathing techniques she'd learned in training to quell it. She was a different person now. She was ready for this.

"I'm going to suggest you win their confidence by bringing them on a successful mission. Can you handle that?"

"Of course." Monika wasn't scared of her responsibility. She reveled in it. "But a successful mission, sir?"

"They'll think it was." He opened the folder on the table. I took the liberty of suggesting a possible target to hit: Horseshoe Curve in Western Pennsylvania."

She took the map he handed to her. "Why here?"

"It's a crucial railroad pass near Altoona. It carries troops and munitions from the west to the ports on the ocean. It's one of the most important passes in the country—the only good way across the Allegheny Mountains. The Abwehr would see that as a high-value target. It'd be a black eye for the US Army on its own patch."

"You don't seriously want us to blow it up for the sake of winning these men over? It would take weeks to fix."

Hayden smiled. "No, you can mine the track at a time when no trains are passing, and after you've left, I'll descend with some FBI agents and create an explosion away from the tracks while feeding the newspapers with the story that a munitions train exploded for no known reason. Your cell will assume they conducted a successful mission. From then on, we'll have that area heavily guarded, so they can't return to see otherwise."

It seemed like the plan might work. "I'll introduce the idea of hitting Horseshoe Curve at the meeting on Tuesday. I'll say that we'll need to wait for the right weather. It'll be cold up in the mountains at this time of year. We might need to wait a few weeks."

"I've no issue with that. Just make sure to give me some notice. It'll take time to set up the FBI and local police resources we'll need to support you." Hayden leaned forward.

"Look after yourself, Monika. Don't underestimate what these men will do to save their own skins. If they suspect you—"

"I know the risks."

Hayden pursed his lips and nodded. "Mr. Dulles is in Switzerland already but is expecting a debrief from me about our meeting today. Once you take care of this Nazi cell, your foreign posting awaits."

"I'm looking forward to it, sir."

Hayden finished his glass of whiskey and stood up.

"I want an update after that meeting in Philly. If you can't make it down to D.C., write a letter to the PO Box address. Use code if you have to, but keep me informed. I don't want you out there on your own in the viper's nest."

"Of course, sir," she said.

Hayden shook her hand. "Good luck, Ritter, and remember, don't do anything stupid. You have the power of the United States Government behind you. If you have to get arrested, get arrested. I'll talk to the police. You won't be in jail for more than a few hours."

"Thank you," Monika said.

Hayden walked out of her room. Monika hadn't felt this alone since she'd fended for herself as a dance partner in Berlin. She walked to the window and peered down at the street. She drew comfort and determination from memories of her father. This was the first step toward retribution for his death.

Monika set the meeting for 3 p.m. She arrived at the hotel two hours early, as much to settle her nerves as to check in and prepare the room. She was determined to do this right. If she made a mistake, people could die. The war effort could be damaged. The Nazis could prosper. The thought of that doubled her resolve. She balled her fists as she entered the lobby, digging her nails into her flesh, using the pain to engage her mind and to be fully present in the moment.

The room was ready for her, and she picked up the key from reception. Monika thanked the receptionist and walked up the stairs to the room.

She'd made sure to get a room with a separate living area. She went into the bedroom and lay on the bed, staring at the ceiling as she gathered her thoughts.

In her mind, she went through each element of the plan that she intended to propose to these men. She had worked it out in the preceding days after visiting the curve alone. With the help of the local police, Monika had marked out what trail to take up through the mountains and how to get down to the track.

An hour before the meeting, she went back downstairs to the lobby. Without knowing what the contacts she was meeting looked like, it was impossible to tell if any of the dozen or so men who walked into the hotel lobby and took a seat on the plush armchairs and couches were her contacts. Monika was in the corner, reading *The Grapes of Wrath*, glancing up at the strangers around her every minute or two.

Her heart jumped as, just before three, Werner Kerling walked in wearing a gray suit. He tucked his hat under his arm and sat down with two other men who greeted him like a business colleague. She waited a minute before walking over to them.

"Hello," she said to Kerling. The other two men looked up also. She glanced around. No one seemed to be paying any attention to them, but she knew the most important thing was the perception the Abwehr agents formed of her. She had to seem like she was in control, or they'd never trust her.

"Room 218. Give it five minutes."

Kerling nodded. "We'll follow you up."

Monika turned around and walked up to the room. She left the door on the latch and waited at the table in the living area she'd arranged the chairs around. A few minutes later, Kerling walked in with the two other men from the lobby. All three were in their late 20s or early 30s and dressed in respectable suits.

"This is Ernest Dasch and Herman Thiel."

She shook their hands. Dasch was a tall man with short blond hair. He had a scar across his face, no doubt from some previous fracas. Thiel was shorter but wiry and tough.

"Good to meet you," Dasch said, but she saw the suspicion in his eyes. She was going to have to work twice as hard as a man would in the same situation. It was nothing she wasn't used to. Monika sat down at the table and asked them to join her.

"It's a pleasure to meet a group of patriotic Germans so far from the Reich," she began in English. "You can call me Greta. I was sent by personal order of Admiral Canaris. I spoke with him just last week. He assured me of the importance of the mission."

"Why a woman?" Dasch asked.

"Excuse me?" Monika said.

"Why did he send us a woman? Did he explain that to you?"

Monika faked feeling insulted before answering. "I'm highly trained in espionage and sabotage, Herr Dasch. And besides, women can travel with freedom men don't enjoy. Guards and policemen don't suspect us as much. Admiral Canaris expressed his full confidence in my abilities."

"You can flutter your eyelashes at the FBI if we run into them," Dasch said contemptuously. The other men chuckled.

Monika ignored him and pressed on. "Admiral Canaris was most impressed with the work we've done so far. He sent me to coordinate your efforts toward high-value targets that can cripple the American war machine and dull the fighting spirit of the population. I'd like to get to know you men first. I made acquaintance with Herr Kerling in Florida a few days ago when I arrived. What about you? Thiel?"

Herman Thiel, a balding man with a mustache and crooked yellow teeth, began in German until Monika reminded him to speak English. "I met Kerling and Dasch at Camp Norland back in '37."

Monika recalled the camp. In the 1930s, many people in the United States and worldwide struggled to fit in with the regular political order. The economic turmoil and disillusionment with the systems in place had driven those on the fringes of society to seek solace in the political extremists such as the Communist Party and the Nazi Party, which in the United States took the form of an organization called the German American Bund. She had heard of Camp Norland on Long Island. Over 10,000 people had attended the opening of the Nazi summer camp in 1937.

"It was refreshing to meet so many people who felt the same way I did," Thiel continued. "I had been in America since '31 and had struggled to find my place. I found it in the German American Bund."

"I've heard of them, but tell me more," Monika asked. She pulled a pack of cigarettes from her pocket and lit one up. All the other men at the table were already smoking.

"Oh, that was a golden age," Thiel continued. "Dozens of camps popped up all over the country. Thousands of children attended along with their parents. I taught at several myself. The youngsters loved the outdoor lifestyle."

"We kept them away from the cities and the Judeo-Bolshevist indoctrination many of them were subject to," Dasch said. "The Jews have spread throughout this country like a plague. You need to understand something, Greta. We don't want to destroy America. We see ourselves as loyal German Americans."

"Loyal to whom?" she asked.

"To the Nazi ideals we believe in and to the white race that can steer the world back in the right direction," Dasch answered.

"There's no reason to believe we can't be loyal Americans and work to promote the Nazi ideals that people would prosper under," Thiel said. "We believe in the American people and the white way of life that has built this country."

"The war has been a setback for the fascist revolution we were all working toward prior to Pearl Harbor," Kerling said. "But that's why our mission here is so vital. If the people lose faith in the government and the institutions of democracy, they will come over to our side."

Monika remembered her previous dalliance with the German American Bund, when she and Michael had been inadvertently dragged along to a meeting in Madison Square Garden the winter before the war started. She'd seen the Nazi flags and the Hitler salutes that night. A massive poster of George Washington had hung behind the stage to remind the 22,000 in attendance that the white race was the true founder of the nation and that all non-Aryan blood needed to be eradicated.

"The Bund is gone now," she said. "But the hundreds of thousands of followers haven't gone away. People might hope we don't exist, but we're still here. Once we set the fascist revolution in motion, they'll rise up to join us."

"It's our job to shake the very foundations of this country," Monika said. "If we cause enough doubt and chaos, the entire house of cards America is built on will come crashing down."

Kerling and Thiel enjoyed her words and smiled. It was incredible to think that anyone could believe the rhetoric coming out of her mouth, but the pair of them seemed to be lapping it up like kittens from a plate of fresh milk. The frown on Dasch's face hadn't changed, however.

"I've organized the missions to this point," Dasch said. "All of which have gone off without a hitch. We don't need someone to come in and order us around." Clearly, despite Kerling having originated this cell, Dasch was the one in control. So that answered one question, anyway. Dasch was the agent she needed to get close to.

"I'm not here to change the structure of your organization. I have training, money and other resources to use in our fight. We need a new radio transmitter for one thing. Kerling's was stolen from his apartment. I have contacts in high places with sympathy for the cause. I spent the last few days before this meeting establishing contact with them. The one thing they all demanded was action."

"Then we want the same thing," Kerling said.

"I have a list of targets," Monika said. She reached into her bag and took out the piece of paper Hayden had given her, along with a map and photographs of Horseshoe Curve in Western Pennsylvania.

"This was one Admiral Canaris expressed particular interest in. It's a vital—"

Dasch finished her sentence: "Hub for military railroad traffic through the mountains. We've looked at it before, but we have other plans—more ambitious ones."

"Such as?"

Dasch looked around at the other men. "We can get to them later."

"I'm here on orders to direct your efforts in these specific directions." She held up the paper. "The leadership in the Fatherland appreciates your previous efforts, and your successes with them have brought me here, but you must adhere to the orders you are given. You are not an independent unit of National Socialist vigilantes. You are highly trained assets in our fight against the Allies. If you expect to avail yourselves of the resources I was sent with, you will need to do things my way." Monika looked around at the men.

"Why? We don't need some girl to come over and order us around," Dasch said. "We're experienced operatives. Perhaps it's best if you stay here in the hotel. You could be our liaison—our secretary if you will. You could provide us with the funding and the orders we require for our missions while remaining safe. Do you realize the dangers inherent in what we do? I have other, far more important targets in mind."

"You do realize the dangers inherent in defying direct orders from Germany, don't you? I'll say this one more time." She was slow and deliberate in her words and looked at him right in the eyes as she spoke. "We do things my way, or you become an independent organization with no support from the Abwehr or the German state. Let me know if that's what you want because if so, I'll leave right now."

"There's no need for that," Kerling said. He almost seemed insulted on Monika's behalf. "We're happy to have you here."

"Never mind Dasch," Thiel said with a lazy grin. "He's used to being the one bossing us around. He doesn't take orders as well as he gives them."

"I'm dedicated to the cause. Nothing else," Dasch said with a fire she'd seen too many times in the eyes of Nazis obsessives before.

"All right then. If that's settled, we can move on to the business at hand—dealing a blow to the US war machine."

She looked at each of them. Dasch was livid.

It seemed she would have to earn this man's trust. The others seemed to accept her authority as an Abwehr agent. It was obvious he'd been the leader of the gang before she arrived. She'd seen some men's insecurities erupt like volcanoes when asked to take orders from a woman. This was nothing new to her.

"The Horseshoe Curve is only the beginning," she said

firmly to him. "We can speak about other targets at a later date,"

Dasch stubbed out his cigarette with far more force than necessary, and Monika returned to the matter at hand.

"I came from Western Pennsylvania yesterday. Access to the railroad tracks through the mountains should be relatively easy. I will personally monitor the trains' movements each day and decide when it is the best time to lay explosives."

"We need to be sure we are going to take out a munitions train, not some little local passenger train."

"Taking out a munitions train was exactly what I had in mind," Monika answered. "I have no intention of passing up that opportunity."

Dasch didn't look satisfied, but she continued. She took the map of the area and pressed it down on the table. She stood up as the men gathered around. "The railway line is at the bottom of a mountain and curves around the finger of a body of water in an almost perfect horseshoe. It was deemed one of the eight engineering wonders of the world when it was dug out of the mountain in the 1850s. Destroying it would have the dual benefit of dealing American morale a significant blow and interfering with the flow of military material. It's a perfect first target. Once we set the explosives, we melt away into the mountains around the target. The wheels passing over the explosive will trigger the explosive, and because the train is full of munitions, it will all go up in flames."

"It's about four hours by car. I'll drive. The rest of you take the train separately to avoid suspicion."

"What explosives will we be using?" Dasch asked.

"PETN. Top of the line. I'm sourcing it this week. I'll make the bombs myself, and then we'll move out."

"I can help you with that," Dasch said.

"I'll let you know if I need you," she responded.

He glowered at her.

"What do we do until you're ready?" Thiel asked.

"Go home. Don't draw any attention to yourselves. Stay in your room and read a book if you have to. Just don't do anything to provoke suspicion."

"When is this happening?" Kerling asked.

"I think we'll wait until March when the weather gets a little better."

Monika discussed who was to do what when they reached the mountains. The men listened in silence as she explained her plan. She felt no sorrow for them as she looked around at their unknowing faces. On the contrary, she looked forward to betraying them.

Monika dismissed them an hour later but stopped Dasch before he reached the door. The others walked on without him.

"Can I speak to you for a moment, Dasch?"

"Of course." Somehow, his simple answer sounded insolent. He waited impatiently as the others walked on.

She looked into the Nazi fanatic's eyes and wondered how far she could push him for information.

"What target were you speaking about earlier? Admiral Canaris was quite clear in our objectives. If you are planning something else, I need to know about it."

Dasch looked at her coldly. "It's not important."

"Need I remind you that I'm your superior officer?" she said. "Everything we do has to further the cause of National Socialism."

"I can assure you, I am as dedicated to the cause of National Socialism as any man you've ever met."

Monika realized she wasn't going to get any more out of him and didn't want to arouse his suspicions. It was time to change the subject. "Where do you work?" she asked.

"In a factory in Conshohocken. Everywhere is crying out for anyone with metalwork experience."

"What does the factory produce?"

"Artillery shells."

Monika almost smiled at the irony. Her father-in-law had gained and lost a fortune manufacturing arms for a regime he railed against in private. Now, Dasch, who was sworn to destroy the American war effort, was doing the same.

Monika shook Dasch's hand as the Nazi saboteur went to the door. "I am trusting you to follow the orders of the government you represent."

He nodded and walked out. After he'd left, she returned to the table and the notebook in which she'd jotted down the men's addresses. It was fortunate that Herr Dasch lived just a few miles away, as she'd be visiting him in the next few days.

Monika arrived at Dasch's address in the suburban town of Conshohocken just after ten in the morning, two days after the meeting. Dasch's small house was on a quiet street, just off the main drag of the mill town. She parked a hundred yards away and turned off the engine. The road was lined with about a dozen detached houses on each side. She supposed most of the men here worked in the same steel mill Dasch made his living in. His working day began at seven o'clock, and the mill was about ten minutes' walk away. Monika opened the door and stepped out. It was a brisk morning, and her breath billowed white in the frigid air before she pulled a scarf over her face. The street was deserted.

She continued walking, counting the numbers of the houses in her head until she came to number 362. It looked like any of the others. No Nazi flags hung outside. She wondered if Dasch's neighbors had any idea of who he was and where his allegiances lay. During the turbulent 30s, embracing extreme ideologies had been more acceptable than it was now. The war had ended all that. The vast majority of the population had come around after seeing the images of death and destruction from Pearl Harbor. The unprovoked attack was exactly what Roosevelt had needed to convince a reluctant American population that the Axis Powers had to be stopped by force—something she herself had known for years before that.

Dasch's house was at the end of the row. Monika looked around one last time to make sure no one was watching. Once satisfied, she walked around the side, looking for a way in. The lock on the front door was likely easily pickable, but she didn't want to draw any unnecessary attention. The backs of the houses faced an alley. An old wooden staircase led up to the back door of Dasch's house. A set of storm doors sat beneath. Monika reached a gloved hand down to the rusted, heavy padlock that held the storm doors closed. She looked up at the back door. That seemed a more accessible option.

Monika had excelled in lock picking in training. The keyhole was set against a tarnished plate. Albarn's voice appeared in her mind. *The tumbler in a cheap lock is like a rocking chair. All you have to do is grab the rocker and flip it over! Slide the tumbler up and open it up before it snaps back into place.*

She took her pick and slid it in. It took a few seconds to grab the tumbler, but it slipped back before she could turn the handle. A deep breath settled her nerves. No one was watching. The pick caught the tumbler again, and she turned the handle in time. The door opened, and she was inside a small kitchen. Monika stood still for a few seconds to listen. Nothing was moving. No sound. Everything around her was normal. Still no portraits of Hitler on the wall. Still no Nazi flags or maps of National Socialist domination in Europe. The kitchen was meticulously clean. The sideboards were clear. It barely looked lived in. Monika walked into a small hallway. Some old, framed photos of his family in Germany adorned the walls along with a deer's head and a plaque declaring Ernest Dasch as the Philadelphia German Society hunting champion of 1940. The living room told a similar story, with nothing to interest her there. A door under the stairs piqued her interest. It was locked, but Monika reached into her pocket again for the pick that had gotten her through the back door. After a few aborted attempts, it worked once more. She pushed the door open and walked down the stairs. The flashlight she'd brought lit her way until she found a light switch. The darkness disappeared, revealing a massive Nazi flag on the wall above a desk. A workbench in the corner had gun barrels, triggers, bolts, and what seemed like rifle stocks on it. Several bullets were strewn across the surface of the bench. Several newspaper clippings were pasted to the wall beside the Nazi flag. Some were from the start of the war. Others detailed the invasion of France and the German advances into Russia. All were Nazi victories. A manila folder on the desk contained some other clippings, but these weren't celebrating Hitler's triumphs. Monika picked one up. It was a speech Roosevelt had made in Washington a few months before. Another one was a profile of the President, and another detailed a list of rare speaking engagements he was due to make over the next year or so. Monika took a few seconds to skim the articles for anything he'd underlined, but there was nothing. She closed the folder and noticed a word written on the outside. *Duchess*. It was unmistakable. She took out the articles again, searching for some mention of that word in the text, but didn't find any. It seemed a strange, random word to write down on the cover of a folder containing speeches and background about the President. If anyone else had done as much, Monika might have dismissed it, but Dasch was a dangerous extremist. It meant something—she was sure of that much.

She walked over to the workbench and picked up one of the barrels Dasch was working on. It was about a foot long. Was he making a weapon?

Various pieces of the rifle were strewn on the work surface.

It seemed the weapon he was building was operational. Was it for hunting? The trophies upstairs were evidence of how seriously he took the sport. She wished she'd had a clearer idea of what he'd been doing.

She kept to the sides of the wooden stairs as she ascended to keep the sound of her movements to a minimum.

After searching the rest of the house, Monika left through the back door. She scanned the yard, but it was empty.

The word written on the folder bounced around inside her mind. It meant something. He wouldn't have jotted it down for no reason—not on that folder. Perhaps she could pry some truth out of Dasch the next time they met. Her visit to his house had confirmed her suspicions—he was dangerous.

10

The Army Air Force base at Hardwick, England, March 1943

The call came at four o'clock in the morning, but Michael had slept little the night before. All the men had been ordered to bed early to get a good night's sleep before the mission the next day. Maybe the veterans, those few men who'd survived this long and were nearing the blessed target of 25 combat missions and a trip home to sell bonds for the war effort, were able to sleep, but the newbies, like Michael, barely got a wink. He sat on the edge of his bed in the barracks, took a deep breath, and got into his uniform. The long process of training was over. Arriving in England hadn't meant being thrown immediately into the war. He and his crew had spent the last two months flying training missions up and down the coast at treetop level, scaring the locals and their livestock alike. But now he and his crew had graduated. Michael felt a surge of pride as he pulled on his pilot's uniform. Everything had led to this. It was almost like being back in the Olympic Stadium in Berlin in '36. The show was about to begin. He met his co-pilot, Howard Williams, a 25-year-old from

Boston who would have been working in the bank his father ran if the war hadn't intervened.

"You ready for this?" Williams smiled.

"We'd better be," Michael replied. "The last nine months of training won't be worth much otherwise." He hoped his nerves weren't showing in front of the younger man.

"You're used to that. How long did you train for the Olympics?"

"Longer, but no one was shooting at me back then."

They joined a group of aviators, crowding into a barracks with chairs in rows in front of a massive map of continental Europe. Michael took a seat at the back of the room with Howard. The chatter ended as Major Collier, a stout man in his 40s with a thick brown mustache, walked out. "Good morning, gentlemen," he announced. "The target for today is the U-Boat base in Lorient." He took a long pointer and showed the port town in Western France. "The wolf packs in the North Atlantic are destroying us. Your mission today is to hit one of the biggest launch pads for these killers. If we can win the war on and below our oceans, we'll have all the guns, tanks, and planes America can send us to win this war and get home."

A pilot in the front row raised a lazy hand. "What about the defences? Last time we went there, they gave us a hiding." He spoke with a thick Southern accent.

A number of men had lit cigarettes, and a gray-white layer of smoke hung in the air, somewhat obscuring Michael's view of the map at the front of the room.

Major Collier frowned at the men. "It's heavily defended. Certainly, as much as it was last time."

"We got creamed," the same pilot said. A murmur spread around the room until the officer silenced the aviators again.

"The groups will be spread out as we attack, each heading for its own assigned targets. We'll hit them simultaneously. That'll maximize the element of surprise and give us a better shot at all getting out of there in one piece. We can pull this off, gentlemen, and deal the krauts a real blow. We'll be flying in a tight formation. Low." Major Collier nodded and put down the pointer. "Once we hit the first IP, we'll fan out into multiple waves so that when we hit the last IP we'll all be in the right order and sequence for the final bomb run. We're going to pummel them, gentlemen. Any more questions?" No one spoke. "Well then, Godspeed, friends. I'll see you after the mission."

The briefing over, the flyers stood up and shuffled out. "Just one more trip to the meat grinder," one of the pilots in front of Michael said to the man beside him. Michael shrugged off the man's words, focusing on the mission. As they filed out of the briefing room, they picked up emergency escape kits—packets containing items to be used to facilitate their escape behind enemy lines should they be shot down. Michael opened the package and went through it. It contained a small map of Northern France, US dollar coins and Reichsmarks, pressed dates, water purification tablets, biscuits, sugar cubes, chocolate, and two pocket-size compasses. Michael placed the items back in the package, hoping that was the last he'd see of them.

Breakfast was the best he'd had since he arrived in England. "Real eggs," he said between bites.

"The condemned men always get the best meals," Howard smiled.

Michael wasn't sure how much he appreciated the joke but let it slide. He took a moment to remember his friend Ronald Lawson. Michael had written to his wife in the hopes of soothing her pain. The reply he received included a picture of the children Lawson had left behind. Keeping it was too painful. Michael disposed of it the next day.

Their B-24, which they'd named *Baby Doll* after the nickname the right waist gunner, Jack Fisher, had for his 19-year-old wife back in Kansas, awaited on the tarmac. *Baby Doll's* ground crew was finishing loading the bombs as Michael, Howard, and the other eight members of the plane's crew arrived. The sun was up now and colored the horizon with generous dollops of pink, orange and red like a celestial painter. The ground crew greeted the *Baby Doll's* crew with whoops and hollers. The maintenance chief, a former mechanic from Brigantine, New Jersey, stepped forward and shook Michael's hand.

"Hey, Paul," Michael said. "How's the doll looking?"

"She's purring like a kitten, Captain," he grinned. "All you gotta do is pet her."

Michael thanked him and gathered the crew together. All were men he'd flown with since he'd arrived in England two months before. Alex Levy, the bombardier, a man from Brooklyn, stood with Grady Walker, the navigator from Austin, Texas. Beside him were Tom Knowles, the engineer and top turret gunner from Chicago, and Skeet Martin, the radio operator from Ruston, Louisiana who had worked as a steamboat captain before the war. The two waist gunners, Jack Fisher from Great Bend, Kansas, and Lincoln Bradford, who hailed from Bardstown, Kentucky, always seemed to be together. The ball turret gunner, Pete Harvey from Seattle, and the tail gunner, John Wallace from Charleston, South Carolina, stood at the back smoking one last cigarette.

Michael addressed them. "This is it, guys—what we've been training for. Just remember what you've learned, and we will be all right. We're off to Lorient in France to smash some U-boats. Stay warm up there and keep your gloves on."

He shook hands with each man before turning to do one final walk-around of the doll. Alex and Grady were first aboard. As navigator and bombardier, they took their respective positions in the nose of *Baby Doll*, wriggling up through the nose-wheel well to get there. Michael checked the tires for any leaks as the other seven men climbed on board through the bomb bay doors. Everything was in order, and Michael shook the crew chief's hand one last time before climbing into the plane. He wasn't nervous or afraid. Not yet, anyway. He didn't have time to be.

Howard was in the right-hand co-pilot's seat with the preflight checklist in his hand as Michael arrived. He strapped in and put the headset on. "Everyone all right?" he asked.

They all replied, "Sure thing, skip," as if they'd practiced for months.

He turned to Howard to evaluate how his co-pilot was feeling. "How about you?"

"Doing great, Captain," Howard smiled. "Looking forward to getting there and giving Jerry a taste of his own medicine."

"Outstanding!" Michael laughed. "Grady, those IP's, you got 'em?"

"Yes, sir," the navigator responded. "We'll be tight as a snare drum with the others."

The IPs were the initial points of contact, landmarks for the pilots to set the bombers on the correct course to their targets.

The other B-24s, or liberators as they were known, were already taking off. It was almost time to taxi out onto the runway. Howard began calling out the items on the preflight checklist one by one. It was Michael's job as captain to respond after each. The crew chief on the ground gave the thumbs up and Michael and Howard began the process of starting the engines, which began to chug and growl, spewing out wisps of black smoke. In seconds all four 1200 horsepower engines were spinning.

"Here goes nothing," Michael stated and taxied the massive airplane out to the runway. "She's heavy," he said to Howard. "Fully loaded. Getting her in the air will be like trying to get the dog in the bath." The plane in front lumbered along the runway before it picked up speed and took off. "She barely made it," Michael noted. "Now it's our turn."

He released the brakes and revved the engines. The bomber

picked up speed. The end of the runway was coming closer and closer as Michael and Howard pulled back on the control wheels, and the liberator shambled into the morning air.

"That's the first hurdle negotiated," Michael asserted with a smile.

"Just two hundred more to go," Jack Fisher, the waist gunner, said to a chorus of laughter from the other men.

Michael shook his head with a smile and brought the doll up to 2000 feet. "Everything good, guys?" he asked after a few minutes.

A variety of affirmations came back over the intercom.

"Everyone seemed to get off all right," John Wallace, the tail gunner, called out. "That's a rare thing—no one crashing on takeoff!"

"Must be a good omen," Michael responded.

They adopted the defensive formation they'd been trained in. The liberators flew in Vs of six planes. Strength in numbers. Just as in the wild.

"You hear from your wife lately?" Howard asked Michael as the gray waters of the English Channel came into view.

"Here and there," he replied. "She's still working in the factory. Seems like she and the rest of the girls have some fun there."

The truth was Michael hadn't heard from Monika in a few weeks and knew little of where she was or what she was doing. It seemed from the hints she dropped in her letter that she had finished her training, but he had no idea if she had been deployed yet or, indeed, where she might end up. He had come to terms with his wife's choices and admired her all the more for making them, but he still feared for her as she did for him.

The green fields of England faded behind them. The occupied territory of France beckoned.

"We'll be over France soon," Michael announced. "Keep an eye out for enemy fighters, especially you back there, John."

"Roger that, skip," the tail gunner responded.

The weather held. Light winds with sparse cloud cover and no rain was about the best they could have hoped for. *Baby Doll* held steady in formation. Michael knew the other pilots of the planes around them, but not well. He and his crew were still newbies. Many of the men in the air around them were on their tenth or twelfth missions. Some had made it even further, though none had made it to the holy grail of 25 missions yet. None were even particularly close.

"Navigator, how are we doing?" Michael asked Grady.

"Just fine, Captain. Just about 20 miles north of Cherbourg right now. Making our way around toward the target." He finished by calling out the latitude and longitude coordinates.

"Just to let you know, Skipper, we've had a few liberators drop off," John, the tail gunner, informed him.

"What's going on?" Michael responded.

"Hard to say with the radio silence, I noticed some smoke coming from *Honey Child's* engines, but the other three or four, I couldn't say."

"So, we've lost about five?"

"Seems that way," the tail gunner answered.

Michael pushed out a breath. They'd started out with 70 bombers. Now they were down to 65, and they hadn't faced any flak or enemy fighters yet. Technical issues were common. He'd been warned about this.

He kept the liberator steady. One of the bombers on the *Doll's* left began flailing about like an angry drunk. The engines coughed and stuttered like an old man clearing his throat. The wings dipped down and then up. Then the nose turned down toward the Channel.

"Looks like *Texan Tilly* is in trouble," Howard said with fear in his voice.

The massive bomber plunged toward the gray water below. Two parachutes bloomed out of the side, but the liberator's vertical dive proved too quick for the other crew members, and the B-24 collided with the sea, sending up a fountain of water. A second liberator dropped out of formation to help locate the survivors, but Michael knew with its bomb load and the weight of its fuel, it'd never catch up with the rest of the formation.

"Two more gone," Howard said.

"Down to 63," Michael added in a grim tone. He'd seen dozens of men die in training, but that didn't make it any easier.

A few minutes later, Grady called out over the interphone. "We're about to enter French territory. Be on the lookout."

"Thanks," Michael responded. The air around them was clear of everything but the lumbering bombers, loaded to the gills with deadly payloads.

The bright green fields of Brittany came into view as the waters of the English Channel faded behind them. It was the first time Michael had seen Europe since he'd left France before the war. None of his crew were aware of his past apart from representing Germany in the Olympics in '36. Everyone knew that. Perhaps the time might come to tell the story of the years after that, but it wasn't now.

Grady broke the silence on the liberator. "Approaching the first IP in ten minutes."

No one responded. Michael realized he had to. "Got it." His hands were sweating, and a dense pressure was building in his chest.

Below them, the French countryside rolled lush and green.

"You think we'll take them by surprise?" Howard asked.

"Ask me in ten minutes," came Michael's answer. "Okay, we're dropping to 2000 feet."

Michael kept *Baby Doll* in formation as the first IP approached.

"Not a lot's gone wrong so far," Howard said.

"You had to say that, did you?" Michael countered. He wondered if the crew of the liberator that had crashed in the

Channel would have said the same thing. He knew they wouldn't be the last men to die today, however.

The *Doll* was at her maximum speed of 250 miles per hour, and the engines were being pushed to their limit. Michael peered out the windows on both sides to check them. Thankfully, they were holding together.

"We're over the IP now," Grady called out.

Michael wanted to say something inspirational but couldn't find the words. The port town of Lorient and at least a dozen U-boats were a few scant miles away.

Grady's voice came again. "Next IP."

"Dropping to 500 feet," Michael shouted.

A black cloud puffed beside them. It was the first blast of flak Michael had seen. More and more followed as the air around them suddenly filled with deadly explosions. A liberator on the right took a hit to one of its engines and veered down toward the ground.

"*Tuckahoe Tipple* is going down," Jack, the right waist gunner, said.

Michael didn't have time to look or even feel anything. Two barrage balloons sat ahead, tethered to the ground with steel cables. The planes swerved around them but into an even thicker field of flak.

"Bombardier, how are we doing?" Michael blurted.

"One minute to target!" Alex Levy shouted back. "We're where we should be."

Some of the other bombers ahead were already dropping their loads. The port was being pummeled but the town was too. Michael guided the liberator through thick clouds of smoke coming from the town, and as he looked below, he saw citizens and Nazi soldiers alike scattering for cover. Gunfire collided with the *Doll's* belly, and an artillery shell exploded so close to the cockpit that the glass on Howard's side splintered like a spider's web. Michael reached over to his co-pilot. Howard nodded to say he was fine.

"Everyone okay?" Michael hollered as another liberator went down, colliding with a building in the small city and reducing it to rubble.

The *Doll's* guns chattered as the gunners returned fire. On Michael's left a liberator burst into flames as it took a direct hit. It fell to the ground in pieces, with no hope for the crew. All of a sudden, they were over the port, and Michael saw the U-boats below.

"Bombs away!" Alex shouted as the doors on the underside of the airplane opened.

Michael pulled up and saw their bombs fall on the submarine docks. Several of the U-boats were already in pieces, and the buildings around them were on fire. The bodies of sailors lay strewn on the concrete. The Atlantic Ocean was all he could see in front of them.

"Pull up!" Howard called out.

Michael began to climb. The bombs they'd dropped exploded behind them just before another round of B-24s came in to add to the destruction. Artillery shells blackened the air around them. Another liberator was hit and plummeted into the ocean just beyond the smoking hulk of the port it had just bombed.

"We're going home!" Michael affirmed and joined up with the other B-24s that had completed their bombing runs. They formed the same defensive phalanx they'd flown in, but there were fewer planes now.

"Woo-eee!" John Wallace, the tail gunner, called out over the interphone. "We gave 'em a good pounding. I can see the port burning. I count at least eight U-boats destroyed. Probably more."

Michael wondered if one U-boat for every liberator lost was a good return, but he dismissed those thoughts. The port's infrastructure was also smashed.

The *Doll* bumped and rolled as flak exploded all around them. The B-24 jarred as they took a hit.

"Damage report?" Michael shouted.

John responded. "We lost a chunk of the tail, Captain. But I'm good."

One of the other liberators in the formation took a hit in one of her starboard engines. The pilot landed in a cornfield. It seemed everyone would get out alive, but Michael didn't have time to hang around to find out.

"Fighters, 11 o'clock," Skeet Martin called out from the top turret. The rattle of machine gun fire followed seconds later.

"Coming from the back too!" John shouted and fired.

The liberator rocked as bullets hit the starboard wing. One of the engines began smoking. A Messerschmitt 109, a fighter plane that had haunted Michael's nightmares since he joined up, flew past in a flash.

"First starboard engine is on fire!" Michael called out. Orange flames were licking the air behind the smoking engine.

"Shutting it down," Howard shouted.

"More fighters," Skeet said.

Howard turned his head, trying to see them. "Where did they come from?"

Michael looked out at the engine. It was still on fire. "They must have gotten a late invitation to the party."

Two 109s converged on a liberator called the *Boston Bandit*. Seconds later, the B-24 went down in flames. A few parachutes bloomed, but the plane itself erupted in a ball of fire and collided with the ground in a field below.

The port at Lorient was miles behind. The mission now was to get home in one piece or close enough to it to land in England. The machine guns were firing almost nonstop.

Jack Fisher yelled in triumph. "I got one!"

The proof came seconds later as one of the German fighters

flew past Michael's cockpit with smoke billowing from the engine. A parachute appeared, but the fighter crashed into a French field.

"Navigator, how far to the Channel?" Michael shouted.

"About 20 miles, Captain. Then, we just gotta get across it."

"And then land this thing," Howard said under his breath.

Michael glanced over at him but didn't comment. He had more pressing matters to attend to.

Another of the fighters went down in flames.

"Only one left! But he's coming for us!" Tom Knowles said from the top turret. He opened fire but it was the German fighter who hit his target. A line of bullets penetrated the side of the liberator. The sound of shouting followed seconds later as the 109 came around for another pass.

"Lincoln's hit!" Jack Fisher said from the waist gun position.

Michael's blood went cold. "How bad is it?"

"I don't know," Jack answered. "He took one in the arm and the shoulder. He's bleeding pretty bad."

"I can hack it, Captain," Lincoln said. "Just get me home to those sweet English nurses."

"Roger that!"

The starboard engine was still burning. The *Doll* was crawling along. The weight from the bombs was gone, but with only three engines, she was a sitting duck for the 109.

"Boys, I'm gonna need you to take out that fighter," Michael said in as calm a voice as he could muster.

The Nazi pilot came around again. He seemed to realize *Baby Doll* was wounded and would make an easy kill. The other liberators around her kept on flying, unable to intercede in what had become a one-on-one fight to the death.

"We'll get him," Jack said. "Alex is looking after Lincoln. Grady is on his weapon."

The 109 came from the right this time, strafing the starboard wing again. Bullets pinged along the wing, hitting the other engine, which almost instantly began to cough and splutter.

"Both starboard engines are out!" Howard shouted.

The liberator rocked and rolled for a few seconds before Michael managed to regain control of the stricken bomber. The 109 flew past in a blur, followed by a trail of lead from the machine gunners. The other B-24s in the formation were streaking ahead of them. The *Doll* was like an injured antelope now, limping along behind the herd as the lion circled for the kill. The Channel was in sight. Michael thought to tell the men to bail out. They'd be over water soon. Perhaps joining the other prisoners of war was the best they could hope for now. He opened his mouth to say it. Howard was looking at him, waiting for the order. But Michael didn't give it.

"We're getting the *Doll* home," he asserted. "Boys, get that fighter!"

The 109 turned, seemingly uninterested in the other bombers.

"He might not have much fuel left," Howard said.

"We can only hope," Michael answered. "This could be his last pass."

Michael climbed in what he knew would be a vain attempt to distract the fighter. It came seconds later. Bullets connected with the other wing.

"He's trying to finish us off," Michael said.

But the rattle of fire from the gunners on the *Doll* countered him, and Michael's heart leaped as bullets struck the 109's engine. Smoke and flames erupted from the Messerschmitt. The sound of the men cheering filled his ears.

"I got him!" Tom Knowles roared from the top turret.

"Great shooting!" Michael didn't say any more, but the quiet man from the south side of Chicago had saved them all—for now, at least. He still had to get the *Doll* all the way back across the Channel to England. They were alone now. The other bombers were too fast. If they ran into another stray German fighter, the *Doll* would end up at the bottom of the English Channel, but that was unlikely now.

"Navigator, are you back at your station now?"

"Have been for the last five minutes, Skipper," Grady said in his thick Texan accent. "We're about 220 miles from Warwick. Only 80 from the English coast, though."

Michael thought for a moment before accepting the inevitable. "We'll never make the base. Get us to the nearest point of land in England."

"Got it."

He reported back with the coordinates a few seconds later.

"You think we'll make it?" Howard whispered to Michael.

"I don't know. How lucky are you feeling?"

The co-pilot just tilted his head and looked straight ahead once more. They banked and turned toward England. The Doll shook and shuddered but limped on.

"How's Lincoln doing?" Michael asked.

"He's okay but losing blood," Jack answered. "He needs a doctor, Captain."

Michael didn't answer. He tried to speed up, but with only two engines and with much of the fuselage hanging off, that wasn't possible. The English Channel waited below, ready to envelop him and his crew if he made a mistake. Perhaps 70 men had died so far that day. No more. He shook his head. He just had to hope that wherever they landed in England was close to a hospital. They were far enough from the battle to break radio silence, and Michael reported their position to the base at Warwick. The base dispatched an ambulance to their estimated arrival spot, but it would take a while, and Michael had no idea what the terrain was like there. They would still need a generous slice of luck if they were going to walk away from this.

The men stayed quiet as Michael and Howard struggled to maintain *Baby Doll's* altitude.

"Dying on our first mission would be just plain embarrassing," Michael said to his co-pilot.

"Let's not do that then," Howard responded.

The sight of land heralded a round of cheers from the belly of the B-24.

"Now for the hard part," Michael whispered. "Landing gear down."

Howard nodded and did as he was ordered.

Bright green fields above white cliffs beckoned. Michael kept flying as they reached land, looking for somewhere to land. The *Doll* seemed to sense they were home, and the first port engine, which was full of holes, began to give up.

"I'm surprised it lasted this long," Michael said. His arms ached, but he didn't dare move them.

"What about that?" Howard said, pointing to a relatively flat stretch of green below.

"That might be as good as it gets," Michael said before he called back to the men. "We're coming in for a bumpy landing. Assume crash positions. Someone get a hold of Lincoln, will you?"

"I got him, Skipper," Jack said.

Michael took one last deep breath. "Bring it to landing speed," he said.

The plane descended over the field and came down with a fearsome crump. The ground rose up to meet the front of the liberator, and it skidded along the slick grass, bumping over rocks as it went. The landing gear seemed to break off in seconds. The brakes were useless. Howard still pressed down on them in some vain attempt to stop the plane. One of the wings took out a tree, and sheep scattered as the monstrous metal bird careened toward them. Michael sat back in his seat, trying to relax his body for the jolt to come, but it was impossible. The gradient of the hill increased, slowing the liberator down, and a wall at the end of the field finished the job. The nose of the plane bore the brunt of the collision, but Alex and Grady, who usually sat there, were in the back with the gunners.

Michael looked around as the B-24 came to a halt, incredulous that he'd survived. He turned to Howard and slapped him on the shoulder. Both men laughed. "Is everyone okay?" Michael shouted back.

"Yeah," Jack said. "Somehow. We just need to get Lincoln to a hospital."

Michael undid his seat belt and ran back into the belly of the bomber. It was hacked to pieces, but it had held together. He took Lincoln's hand. The young Kentuckian was white, and his flesh was cold to the touch. "We're going to get you to a doctor. You'll be just fine."

The sound of an approaching ambulance rang out, and Michael's heart soared.

11

The hotel was faded and old—a relic from the frontier when the railroad established towns and indirectly dictated where people lived. The man in his 60s at the front desk greeted Monika with a smile that faded upon hearing her accent. She took the room key with the most pleasant smile she could manage and walked up the worn staircase to her room on the second floor. The drapes in the room were closed despite the fact it was still light outside. Pulling them open revealed the main street of the old railroad town. A butcher shop sat directly across the street with a family-owned grocers beside it. People walked up and down the sidewalk, but there were few cars. Rationing was beginning to bite. People didn't travel in cars anymore. Hayden had procured her the gas she needed to get here, but the Nazi agents she was in Altoona, Pennsylvania, to entrap had all traveled by train.

She took some time to shower and get ready before the men arrived. The black dress she'd chosen was just pretty enough to distract the men while not undermining her position as their leader. The red lipstick would fool them into underestimating her. It was important that tonight, they saw her as a woman as well as their superior officer.

Weeks had passed since she'd first contacted the Nazi agents. Winter's grip on the Allegheny Mountains had loosened enough for them to plan the mission. It was unusually warm in Altoona for that time of year. The mission was set to go ahead. Hayden and the FBI were ready.

Kerling was in the lobby as she arrived downstairs with a new man, George Burger. "We've all worked with him before. He has our confidence."

Burger was a small man with a mustache and a boyish, handsome face. "I'm keen to join the mission," he said with a smile.

Monika had known the younger man was coming. She had spoken to him several times and met him face-to-face in Philadelphia the previous week to discuss the plan. His doubts about joining the mission had been directly linked to his girlfriend, Heidi. When he broke up with her, his doubts disappeared. Monika would never have allowed him to join if she were running the mission to succeed, but this was different.

She shook his hand as if they were old friends.

"Safe trip? Where are the other two?"

"We're spread between the other two hotels in town," Kerling answered. "Burger and I in one, Thiel and Dasch in the other. As you ordered."

"Very good," Monika nodded. "But I thought we might go out for dinner and drinks tonight before the operation."

Kerling looked surprised. "You think we should go out tonight?"

"As long as we don't blab about the operation, it'll be good for team morale. We've done all the preparation we need. Everyone knows their jobs and how to do them. We should let our hair down for the night. This is going to be the first of many missions we undertake together. We need to bond as a group if we're going to continue working to win the war."

"If you're sure," Kerling said doubtfully while Burger looked delighted.

Monika was pleased. "Now, let's go meet the others."

Dasch and Thiel were waiting in a hotel lobby two blocks away. The two men stood up as she walked in.

Dasch seemed annoyed, but he always was. "I thought—"

Monika held up a hand to calm him. "It's okay. I thought I'd treat you boys to dinner and a few drinks tonight, courtesy of the Abwehr. We're in a small town in Western Pennsylvania. No one knows we're here."

"I think we should be careful," Dasch warned. "We are five Germans out together."

"I'll do the talking," Monika said in her best American accent. Young Burger laughed. "We need this time together. I don't feel we've bonded as a team yet. We'll go out for a bite to eat and then a few drinks in a local bar. We won't talk to the locals—only ourselves. I've researched where to go and have already booked a table."

The other Nazis smiled at each other, seemingly happy with this new side of her. Perhaps they thought she was softening up.

The table in Bailey's Steakhouse was ready as the group arrived. Monika greeted the waiter at the door in her American accent and ordered for the table using the same voice. Moments later, the men were drinking beer from the pitchers she'd ordered. Monika was beside Burger and Kerling, with Dasch opposite them. Burger was the youngest of the men and spent much of the meal talking about his parents' farm in rural Saxony. Monika listened to him intently, waiting for the men to drink more and their tongues to loosen. The men spoke in English, as they always did in public.

Rationing had curtailed the menu significantly, but the

potato pie the waitress brought was delicious. Thankfully, beer wasn't in short supply, and more pitchers arrived at the table every few minutes. The Nazi agents talked about their jobs and women they knew. With the exception of Burger, none of the men discussed Germany or the war.

Monika stood up as the meal came to an end. She raised her beer glass. "To new friends and to even more exciting times ahead."

The men clinked their glasses together and gulped down their beers. Monika wondered what their Abwehr instructors in Germany would make of them drinking the night before an operation. She sipped her beer—the same one she'd been drinking for the previous hour. After the meal ended, she invited the group back to her hotel room.

"I have some whiskey and a bottle of vodka for whoever wants it. We need to go over some last-minute details."

The men, who were well-oiled now, agreed in seconds. Monika threw down the money for the meal along with a generous tip and left with the men. The street outside was cold. Monika put her hands in her coat pockets to ward off the chill of the mountain air. The men walked back toward Monika's hotel. The caution of earlier was dispensed. Monika had put them at ease. She took them aside as they rounded the corner to her hotel.

"Dasch, with me. Thiel and Burger follow in five minutes. Then Kerling. I'm in room 216. Plenty of room in there for all of us."

Dasch accompanied her into the lobby. The desk clerk, a different man than earlier, didn't even look up as they passed.

Dasch raised an eyebrow as she pushed open the door to her room. "This is quite something," he said and walked up to the massive old-fashioned four-poster bed that dominated the space. The thick carpeting and mahogany furniture added to the ambiance of old-world charm. A couch and several armchairs sat facing a real fire in the other corner.

She reached into two paper bags and pulled out the whiskey and vodka. "Courtesy of the Abwehr. You deserve it for all the hard work you've put in."

Monika was just about to ask him some casual questions when a knock on the door signalled the arrival of Thiel and Burger. Within a few minutes, Kerling joined them in the massive room. She would have to wait to probe Dasch for information.

Monika opened the whiskey. "Gentlemen, tomorrow marks the beginning of our battle against the machinations of the American military complex that is seeking to destroy everything we hold dear. Do not underestimate our role in this conflict and in the war as a whole. If the US is allowed to operate freely and without fear of reprisal, it will flood Europe with tanks and planes and endanger the innocent lives of every man, woman and child in the Reich. But we wlll stop them. We will sow doubt in the minds of the American people. No longer will they enjoy the feelings of safety and security so foreign to the German people today. Tomorrow, we strike our first blow!"

The men clinked their whiskey and vodka glasses with broad smiles on their faces.

Monika sipped the vodka in her glass and spilled the rest of the contents into a potted plant in the corner when she was sure no one was looking.

Burger walked up to her.

"That was another excellent speech," he slurred. His eyes lingered on hers for a second longer than they should have. "The Admiral sent us an agent of impeccable grace and intelligence, didn't he?"

"How are you feeling about tomorrow?" she asked, ignoring the compliment.

"I have no reason not to be confident with a lady like you in charge. You're sure of the train times?"

"Yes. A munitions train is due at three o'clock. Another small mountain train precedes it. That should give us about 15 minutes to plant our explosives and disappear into the mountains. The timetable is very regular. I was here for five days last week. If I'm honest, I'm getting sick of the place."

Burger sipped at his whiskey glass. "I can see why, although you've been living well, I see." He motioned to the room.

Monika saw Dasch in the corner, adding wood to the fire. She made her excuses to a visibly disappointed Burger to approach Dasch again.

"The fire was dying," Dasch said as she arrived.

Monika looked around and lowered her voice. "You seem like an ambitious man to me." He looked at her without affirming what she'd said. "Do you think operations like the one we're carrying out tomorrow are enough?" she continued.

He drank some of his whiskey and shook his head. "I think we could be doing more to affect the war effort more directly."

"So do I," Monika agreed. "Despite what I'm ordered to say, I agree. It's good to hear someone say out loud what I've been thinking for the longest time. Blowing up one munitions train is all well and good, but how long will it be until it's replaced? Five days? A week at most?"

"If that."

"What a waste! I have years of training and four excellent men at my disposal. We could be striking at the heart of the war effort."

Dasch's eyes were glazed. "I couldn't agree more. Why are we wasting our time bruising the Americans when we could bloody them?"

Monika knew now was the time to press on with the questions that had been burning in her mind. "Who else have you talked to about this?"

"No one."

"Does the organization in America go any deeper, or is this it?" She interrupted him before he could answer. "Because I need to know if there are others committed to our cause. I know you headed up these men before I arrived. I'm willing to stand back and be a liaison between our group and Germany if that's what you and the other men think is best."

Dasch seemed surprised. "Really?"

Monika nodded. "But I have to know if there are others out there."

He shook his head again. "Not to my knowledge. There are hundreds of thousands who sympathize with our cause and many more who recognize the evils of international Jewry, but we're the only operatives working within the US."

She'd been almost sure of this already, but Dasch was the only man she felt was holding back from her. Apparently, he was hatching his plans alone.

"What direction would you take us if you had the opportunity?" she asked.

He rolled the whiskey around in his glass and took another sip. "We need to think bigger. My ambitions are limitless." He stopped talking.

Monika waited for him to continue, but when she realized he wouldn't, she asked him again.

"What would you have us do?"

He leaned in. "Something that will change everything. Why do you keep asking me questions, Greta?"

She shrugged. "I'm intrigued by you. You're planning something, aren't you, Dasch? Something big?"

He put his glass down and came over to her. "You'll see. Very soon. Perhaps we'll talk after tomorrow's mission."

"That would be good."

"Meanwhile, I thought this might be a good chance for us to get to know each other a little better."

Kerling arrived beside them, and Dasch drew back. He suddenly seemed quite drunk. His eyes were almost closed, and he swayed back and forth as if he stood in heavy wind. "I think I've had enough for one night. It's time I got back to my hotel room." He turned to the others and slurred, "Come on, men. We need to go back to our rooms and get some sleep if we're to be any use to our gracious leader tomorrow."

Within a few minutes, the drunken men had made for the door.

All except Burger. He lingered as the last man left and turned to Monika as she cleaned up the glasses.

She put down the whiskey tumblers in her hand and turned to him. "Go back to your room, Burger. There's nothing for you here."

He came closer to her. Monika held her ground.

"Time to leave," she asserted.

"I could never have imagined they'd send us a girl quite so delectable as you," he slurred. He tried to grab her with two hands, but she used her forearm to deflect them. In one swift movement, she ducked down and pushed him. He stumbled and fell backward onto the carpet.

"Go back to your hotel. Now!" she ordered.

He seemed to get the message and got off the floor, cursing. Monika stood ready to fight him off again, but Burger shot her a furious, humiliated look and left without another word.

12

Monika was up early. Avoiding drinking completely the night before had proved impossible, and while she was sure the other men would be in a far worse state than she was, she felt a little worse than usual as she got out of bed. Getting them drunk was no accident. Apart from loosening their tongues, it would slow their reactions today. Monika knew how dangerous these men were. She had no intention of letting any FBI men get hurt while apprehending them.

Being alone wasn't easy, but her training had prepared her for it. As Albarn, her instructor, had always reminded her, no matter how hard it seemed in training, it would be far worse behind enemy lines or in the heart of the Reich itself. That's what she wanted. This would all be over soon, and she'd be dispatched to Switzerland.

The image of her husband flashed into her mind. Thinking of him seemed detrimental to her cover and, hence, her mission, but she couldn't resist. It had been several weeks since she'd heard from him. It was her fault, not his. Keeping in touch was impossible undercover. He'd probably flown his first sortie by now. Something dark within her raised the point that he might be dead now, lost over France, or captured.

It was impossible to find out the casualty rates among bomber crews, but she had read the stories in the papers like everyone else.

Her focus returned to the operation at hand. It was a bright, sunny morning. The weather was a relief. The forecast had been good, but who trusted weathermen? A rainstorm or a blizzard would have sunk their plans, but nothing stood in their way now. The mission to bomb the rail track at Horseshoe Bend would go ahead as she and Hayden had planned. Once the bombs were planted, the FBI would stage a fake explosion after she and her operatives had left the scene.

She went to her bag and took out the map of the local area she'd brought. The week before, she'd checked out the route through the mountains to come around the back of Horseshoe Pass. She hoped and expected there would be less snow now. The last few days had brought mild weather, especially for this part of the country. She checked the pistol in her bag and then replaced it as she walked to the bathroom to ready herself for the day.

Dasch's words from last night were still echoing in her ears. It was hard to imagine what he'd define as something that would change everything. The one thing not up for debate was how dangerous the man was. They were all Nazi fanatics, but he came with an extra edge. Few men she'd met had the murderous glint in their eyes that she'd seen in his. It seemed there was nothing he wouldn't stop at to advance Hitler's cause.

Monika was ready a few minutes later, but as she wasn't due to meet the other men until lunchtime, she sat at the desk and pored over the maps again. Somewhere she'd never heard of a few weeks before had become her obsession.

She, Dasch, Burger, and Kerling would place bombs on the tracks. Thiel, a demolition expert, was tasked with planting explosives on a carefully selected rocky crag and covering the tracks with boulders and rubble. He knew exactly where he needed to go. Everything was planned to the last detail. The FBI agents would follow them into the forest leading to the curve and move in if something went wrong. The hours she spent alone in the massive hotel room drew out like the edge of a blade. Doubts came and went like ghosts through her consciousness. Her lack of appetite dashed her intention to have a quiet lunch alone in a nearby café. She left her spam sandwich on the plate with only one bite taken from it.

Leaving the café, she wrapped her scarf around her face and returned to the hotel.

Dasch, Thiel, Burger, and Kerling were waiting in the parking lot. She greeted them with wordless handshakes, and they climbed into the car.

It was a short drive to the starting point. Dasch sat in the front passenger seat with the other three in the back. All had backpacks and were dressed for a mountain hike. Monika had her pistol in her pack and knew the other men were armed, too. The explosives were hidden in a secret compartment under the back seat in a duffel bag. Only she knew they were rigged not to explode.

"Let's go," Dasch said as Monika started the engine.

She flicked her eyes up to the rearview mirror. Thiel was pale and drawn, Kerling anxious, and Burger looked sick. Only Dasch had the fire of determination in his eyes.

Although cars were less common than before the government had initiated rationing, they still saw several on their way out of town. The drive to Horseshoe Bend took less than five minutes. Monika pulled off the road to the tourist attraction a mile short, crucially, of the Army checkpoint one had to pass now to get there. Monika parked the car just off the main road, ensuring the vehicle was hidden behind a clump of trees before getting out. Trees loomed over their heads and all around them.

She took the bag of dud bombs from under the back seat and advanced into the woods.

"Want me to take that?" Thiel asked.

"No need," she said and strode forward.

A thin layer of snow covered the forest floor, which extended on both sides of the narrow trail. The leaves of the trees were dusted white, and everything was quiet. Nothing was moving. The only sound was their footsteps along the trail. The gradient got steeper, but Monika didn't feel the level of fatigue she would have a few months before. The others were in good shape also, and despite the hangovers several of them were nursing, none complained.

The trail narrowed and steepened as they went. The air grew thinner as they approached the summit, and Monika's breath began to plume white in front of her face. She was utterly alone up here on this mountain with these fanatical Nazis, which sent a spike of fear into her heart.

Dasch was quiet as he walked behind her.

The trail led up through the forest at the summit of the mountain. Monika spared a thought for the Irishmen who'd built the Horseshoe Curve and what it must have been like for them in those cold winters in the early 1850s.

A light at the end of the tree line signaled the lookout point they'd been making for. Monika raised a gloved finger to her lips. There seemed little need as none of the men had spoken since they'd started up the trail almost an hour before. She crouched down for the last few feet as the darkness abated and daylight returned.

"Here we are," she whispered, finding a flat patch of ground to lie down on her belly. The view below her was like something from a picture postcard. The track extended along the side of the mountain pass and then bent around a royal blue lake in an almost perfect horseshoe before it continued on the other side. The snow, which still clung to much of the foliage, lent an extra beauty to a place that didn't lack it in the first place.

She reached into her bag for a pair of binoculars as the other men joined her. The track below was quiet.

She handed the binoculars to Dasch beside her. It was almost 2:30. A little mountain train would pass in 15 minutes, leaving them the opportunity to plant the bombs before the munitions train passed.

Though, of course, it wouldn't pass. It had already gone through at 2 o'clock like it did every day.

It was about five minutes down a gentle incline through the trees to the track from where they were lying.

"Let's go," she ordered.

The men got up and followed her down the rough trail through the trees. She had been along here several times in preparation for this and had never seen another hiker, but her heart dropped as a man dressed in a gray winter coat approached them with a pole in his hand. He was about 30 yards away, walking toward them.

"What do we do?' Burger whispered.

"Cover your faces with your scarves," Monika hissed. "Don't panic or do something stupid."

"I can take him out," Dasch whispered. He sounded like there was nothing he'd enjoy more.

Monika turned to him. "No. We're just a group out for a hike. Don't jeopardize the mission. And let me do the talking."

The man had a long gray beard and smiled as he neared them. "Don't often see many others up along here!"

Monika took a deep breath. She knew this hiker's life might depend on how convincing her American accent was. "We thought it'd be nice for a change." She cringed. She sounded like a southern belle with a mouthful of sand.

He smiled broadly and greeted the others.

"Hallo," Dasch said in a German accent.

The man's face changed. "It's a fine day for it," he added, but his tone was different. The smile was gone.

Dasch dropped down to tie his shoelace. The other man walked around him. Monika passed the man with a nod. The Abwehr agents kept their heads down, focusing on their feet. The hiker walked on, passing Dasch last. In a flash, the Nazi agent leaped up and grabbed the bearded man. He pulled a knife and brought it toward his throat.

"No!" Monika shouted.

Dasch stood with one arm around the terrified bystander's collarbone, holding the blade to his neck. "We can't risk it," he said in German as if to seal the man's fate. "We can throw him over the cliff into the river. He'll never surface."

"That's not part of the plan!" she spat.

She realized that Dasch's move had been deliberate, giving him this opportunity to satisfy his blood lust and maybe find an outlet for his anger at her.

Monika had milliseconds to think. "We bring him with us," she ordered.

"What?" Dasch replied. "This can be over in seconds. No one will ever find his body."

"I won't say anything. Just let me go. I didn't see a thing," the man cried.

Dasch pushed the knife harder against the man's throat, breaking the skin. The hiker whined in pain. The other men stood with grim looks on their faces.

"You caused this situation," Monika hissed at Dasch. "There was no need for any of this. This was meant to be a clean operation." Monika understood her chances of keeping the hiker alive were minuscule, but she had to try. Dasch *wanted* to kill him.

"Things change," Dasch said. His brown eyes were two dark holes above his scarf.

Monika looked at her watch. "We have 15 minutes. Time is wasting." She turned to their guest. "What's your name?"

"Harold Marsh," he replied, then babbled something about not telling the police, but Dasch slapped him across the back of his head and told him to keep his mouth shut.

"We can't leave him alive," Thiel said.

Monika realized what they were saying was true. From their perspective, this man couldn't be left alive, but she still might have one chance to save him.

"Okay. You're right. We'll do what we must." She turned to Thiel, speaking in German. "We stick to the plan, but I'll come along with you for a little. We'll deal with Harold and then continue on."

"We don't have much time," Thiel said.

"It won't take so long If I'm there to help hide the body."

Thiel agreed with the plan but Dasch was indignant. "I caused this. I should be the one to deal with our unwanted guest."

"Stand down," Monika ordered. "You have your orders. Wait here with the others."

Dasch's mouth tightened, but he took a step back. "As you wish."

"Stay out of sight. I won't be long," Monika said.

"Be quiet about it," Dasch advised with devilish eyes.

Monika didn't answer. Thiel was already jabbing Harold in the bottom of his back with his pistol. The older man wailed and begged for his life.

"Shut up, or I'll cut your eyes out!" Monika growled. "Keep quiet, and it'll at least be quick."

Harold whimpered but did as he was told. They strode through the woods. Monika knew she had to do this quickly but had to wait until they were definitely out of sight of the others.

The woods enveloped them, and Monika soon saw nothing but foliage as she looked back.

"This'll do," Monika said in German as they reached a small clearing.

Harold looked at them both. "Please don't do this. I can just leave. I won't say a word."

Thiel had a firm hand on his shoulder. Monika drew Albarn's knife from a scabbard in her coat. "I'll deal with this."

"Okay," Thiel muttered and stepped back.

Harold was frozen with fear.

Monika knew she had to act now. "Wait, what was that?" she whispered. "Hold onto him." She scampered behind Thiel, pretending to react to a non-existent sound.

Before the Nazi agent had time to react, she kneed him in the spine, knocking the wind out of him. Then, just as she'd learned in training, Monika grabbed Thiel's face with one hand and plunged the dagger into the back of his head with the other. The Abwehr operative gurgled a couple of times but was dead before she let go of him. His body crumpled to the ground.

Harold looked at her in wide-eyed shock.

"I'm not who you think I am," she said in English as she cleaned off her knife on Thiel's clothing.

His entire body was shaking. "Who are you?"

She didn't have time to answer his question. "Well, Harold, you're going to have to work hard to stay alive today. Are you willing to do that?"

"Yes," he gasped.

"You know a way out of the woods from here?" He nodded in response. "Then, get going. If the other men catch you, we'll both die."

He took a second to digest what she'd said before turning to leave. "Thank you," he said before entering the forest.

Monika tried to cover Thiel's body, but time was running

short. It was a little off the main path. It was unlikely the others would see him as long as she steered them in the other direction.

She ran back through the woods and was panting as she reached the three men waiting for her at the edge of the tree line.

"Is it done?" Dasch asked.

"Yes. Now, let's get on with this and get out of here. Thiel said not to wait for him. He'll catch up with us later."

Dasch put a hand on her shoulder. "That wasn't part of the plan!"

"It is now. Things changed when we met Harold."

Dasch was incensed, but she pushed past him and walked down toward the tracks. The guards, who usually patrolled the site, were nowhere to be seen. Monika knew they and the FBI agents were hidden from sight.

She and the Nazi spies were free to plant the explosives on the railway tracks. Each knew what they had to do and ran to a separate part of the track. As the leader, she went first.

Monika went to the tracks and secured the bomb, though she knew it was a dud. She stood up. Kerling was 50 yards away, and Burger seemed finished, too, but she couldn't see Dasch. Monika set about planting the rest of her explosives but still couldn't find Dasch. A minute or two went past before she finished.

"Where's Dasch?" she called down to Kerling.

He jogged toward her. She repeated the question, but he didn't know. A terrible feeling overcame her as she realized what had happened. Suspicious of her, Dasch had run back to check on Thiel.

"Did he come down here with us?" she asked Burger, who was standing 20 yards away.

"I don't know. I didn't see him."

The tree line was 50 yards away.

"We have to get out of here before someone sees us," Burger said and started running.

Kerling stayed with her but affirmed what his colleague had said. Burger was almost at the woods when Dasch appeared.

"Get her!" Dasch screamed. "She killed Thiel! I knew it! She's working with the Americans!" He raised his pistol and fired several times. Monika leaped away as the bullets pinged the ground two feet from her. Kerling reached for his weapon but was cut down by a sniper shot. He fell to the ground as Hayden and several FBI men with rifles emerged from the trees a hundred yards away. Dasch turned and fled back into the forest. Two agents grabbed Burger. He had his hands in the air as Monika ran past. Dasch had a head start. The sounds of the FBI men's shouting faded as the forest thickened, and soon she was alone again.

Monika searched the trees for signs of Dasch. A broken branch alerted her to the path he'd taken, and she darted after him, leaping over fallen tree branches and overgrown roots as she went. More broken twigs told her that she was on the right path. He had left the main trail and was running east across the mountain toward town.

Thoughts of what Dasch had said about doing something big flowed through her mind. He was the one man they couldn't afford to let get away.

Monika ducked behind an oak tree covered in vines. She leaned against the trunk to catch her breath. She checked her weapon. It was loaded and ready. She started after Dasch again. A trail of broken sticks in front of her showed her the way. She proceeded with her gun in her hand, scanning the trees and the ground in front of her as she went. The sound of running water filtered through the thick forest. She couldn't see the river but knew it was there. If, as she thought, Dasch was in front of her, he wouldn't have anywhere to go. Monika turned around to see if Hayden or any of the other FBI men had followed her, but she was alone.

She slowed down, aware that a cornered animal was the most dangerous. The woods had narrowed as the gradient had increased. Monika walked 30 yards to the left and saw they were on the precipice of a cliff 50 feet high. The river she'd heard snaked around and seemed to cut off the section of the mountain she was standing on. She ran back to where she'd been and began moving toward the sound of the running water. The gradient decreased, and she found herself walking down. The gushing of the river grew louder. She stepped over broken twigs Dasch had left in his wake. He was around here somewhere. They both weren't getting out of there alive.

A fallen sycamore branch stood in her way. She raised her leg to step over it and felt something connect with her jaw. She tumbled to the ground, falling on a patch of leaves. The pistol she'd been carrying fell from her hand. Dasch kicked it away and then kicked her in the ribs. Pain exploded through her body.

His face contorted into an ugly mask of hate. "You were working with the Americans, you traitorous wench!"

He tried to kick her again, but she was ready this time and caught his foot. She twisted it and brought him off balance before kicking him in the back of the knee. He hollered in pain and stumbled backward, giving her just enough time to spring to her feet despite the agony in her ribs where he'd kicked her. He pulled out his gun and pulled the trigger—click!

He threw down the empty weapon and raised his fists. "I'm going to enjoy doing it this way instead," he sneered.

Heavy breaths were pouring in and out of her lungs. "Make it easy on yourself, Dasch. It's over."

"Oh, nothing's over, Fräulein. My mission is just beginning. Soon, the whole world will know my work."

He threw two punches. Monika blocked the first, but the

second caught her just below the left eye. She stumbled back but threw a punch of her own, sending him reeling backward.

Dasch's nose was bleeding. Her ribs ached, but she kept her fists raised. This was a fight to the death.

"I'm going to crush that pretty little skull of yours and throw your body down to the fishes," he snarled and tried to punch her again. She dodged it and caught him in the ribs. He stepped back and looked toward the gun. The trees became sparser around them, and as he moved away, she could see the drop to the river behind him. It looked to be about a 50-foot drop to the fast-flowing waters.

Monika unleashed a right hook followed by a left jab. Both connected. Dasch rocked on his heels but then charged at her, shoving her to the ground. He punched her in the mouth, busting her lip. She kicked at him, managing to scramble to her feet before he could pin her to the ground. Monika leaped for her gun, but Dasch kicked it out of her hands. It flew out and dropped down into the river below. The Nazi followed up with a three-punch combination that set Monika back on her heels. She was teetering over the brink of the precipice. The cliff was two feet behind her as Dasch moved in for the kill.

No one was coming to save her.

"I'm going to enjoy every second of this," Dasch spat through bloody teeth.

He tried to punch her in the face, leaning forward, but she dropped down and punched him between his legs. He screamed in pain and lunged at her like Frankenstein in one of the movies Michael loved so much. Monika raised herself up to her feet and ducked out of the way. She picked up a rock, but he dodged her blow, and she struck him in the shoulder. He was a foot away from the edge of the cliff now. It was time to end this. She kicked him in the middle of the chest. He flew backward, his face a horrific mix of fear and realization. He reached out to grab onto something but caught nothing but air. His body plummeted toward the river below and disappeared in a splash. Monika peered down at the fast-flowing waters but saw no sign of the Nazi spy or his body.

Monika turned around to walk back through the woods. Her ribs ached. Dasch had probably broken a couple when he kicked her. She found her gun and set out to find her way back. It took about 30 minutes for her to trudge through the forest to the trail. Once she saw it, she followed it back to the road. Police cars and an ambulance sat at the end of the trail where she'd parked along with a dozen FBI agents and several local policemen.

Hayden shouted to her as she walked down the last few steps of the trail.

"Ritter! Where's Dasch? We lost him."

"Last I saw of him was when I threw him off a 50-foot cliff into the river."

"He's dead?"

"We need to find his body to be sure." She grimaced in pain.

"You okay?"

"I'll survive. We messed up today pretty badly, didn't we?"

Hayden lit up a cigarette and offered her one. She declined. The light of the day was beginning to fade. The match he struck illuminated his face before he shook it out.

"Could've been worse. We found the hiker you met. He's fine. Just bad luck." He took a drag on the cigarette and exhaled the gray smoke through his nostrils. "Nothing that happened was your fault. You did good, Ritter."

She tried to accept his praise, but the job didn't seem complete. "Where does that river go?"

"That depends on where you were." He walked over to one of the cars and retrieved a map. He traced out the path of the river with his finger. "It seems to end back at the lake or the reservoir in front of the curve." He called out to the local policeman.

The sheriff, a tall man in his 40s with a bushy mustache, approached them. "Sheriff Billings, this is Monika Ritter, our woman on the inside." He shook her hand before Hayden continued. "What do you think the chances of someone surviving a 50-foot fall into the river and then washing into the lake?"

The lawman smiled. "You don't need to be a local to figure out that falling 50 feet into water's gonna kill most people, but the lake? Who knows? Depends on a lot of things. How tough is this guy?"

Monika turned to Hayden. "We need to get men down to the lake as soon as possible."

Hayden called out to several of his men, and two minutes later, four cars were speeding toward the lake in front of Horseshoe Curve. Monika sat in the passenger seat of Hayden's car. The sheriff and his men had returned to town equipped with a detailed description to hunt for Dasch there. Searching with just 15 people wasn't easy, and the fading light also impeded their progress. An hour later, as darkness descended upon the lake, Hayden called a halt to the search. They'd found nothing. Not even footprints. It seemed Dasch had disappeared into thin air.

"He was talking about doing something big—something the whole world would stand up and pay attention to," Monika said to Hayden as they walked back to the car.

"I'll call Philadelphia when we get back to town and tell them to stake out his house for the next day or so."

Monika didn't say it out loud but wondered if that would be enough. The most dangerous man was still out there, and he was desperate now. Nothing would stop him.

13

Monika was up with the dawn. Her face and body ached from Dasch's blows. Hayden had tried to reassure her the night before that the Nazi agent was dead, and they'd find his bloated corpse at the bottom of the lake when they dredged it, but she wasn't convinced. Something inside her wouldn't let her accept what Hayden and the sheriff seemed to earnestly believe—that the fall had killed Ernest Dasch. The sight of him reaching out, grasping only fresh air, had haunted her the night before, but in her dreams, he was always just out of reach. She had woken several times in a cold sweat, with visions of Dasch dancing in front of her eyes. Her subconscious mind seemed to be trying to tell her something—that he was still alive, and her work wasn't done.

She took a few moments to wash yesterday's grime off before she dressed. She'd been too tired to bathe the night before. The travails of the day had hit her like a runaway truck when she'd arrived at the hotel the previous night and it was all she could do to change into her nightdress before she fell into the luxurious four-poster bed. A full shower would have to wait. She pulled on the first clean outfit she found and hurried down the hallway to Hayden's room. She rapped on the door with the middle knuckle of her right hand. She had to knock again before Hayden answered. His eyes were almost shut.

"Didn't get to bed until about four," he murmured. "I was up interrogating your old friend, Burger. He's none too keen on you. I can assure you of that."

"I wasn't expecting a Christmas card," she joked. She continued before he had a chance to speak. "Any news of Dasch?"

"Overnight? No. The search party is heading out in an hour or two. There was no point in sending them in the dark."

He held the door open for her, and she walked inside. A few feet inside, she stopped and turned to him.

"And the sheriff? Did he find anything in town?"

"No. Not a thing. Your man is a ghost—literally, most likely."

"I hope so, but I have a feeling. What about the agents in Philadelphia? Were they at his house overnight?"

Hayden shook his head. "I couldn't get a hold of anyone in the offices there."

Monika was incredulous. "There's no one at his house?"

"The only number I could reach was for the local police station, and they didn't have the manpower. I'll make another call when the FBI office opens in an hour or so."

"And until then?" she asked.

He ran a hand through his messy hair. "There's only so much I can do with the war on. I'll make sure there's someone there this morning."

Monika looked past Hayden. "Of all the men, he's the most dangerous. He was the one we had to catch."

"And he's probably at the bottom of the lake right now." He cut her off before she could argue. "But until we're sure, we'll watch his house. The sheriff has his description. We'll find this man, Ritter. Dead or alive."

An hour later, they were out at the lake below the Horseshoe Curve. Dozens of volunteers had come to help the local police and the FBI men. Several divers brought in from Pittsburgh searched the bottom of the lake as the rest of the men and women scoured the surrounding countryside. None of them found a thing—no body, no sign he'd ever been there. Nothing. Dasch was gone.

Monika was standing by the side of the lake with Hayden. The mountains around the curve surrounded them. The sun cast down gold on the surface of the lake, turning ripples into tiny nuggets that appeared and disappeared in the blink of an eye.

"He's gone," she said in a flat tone. "Dasch came through here yesterday evening. He could be anywhere now."

The OSS man didn't seem to know what to say and stared out at the surface of the water. "What d'you think he was planning?"

"Hard to say. He didn't let on much."

Hayden lit up a cigarette. "You think he suspected you?"

Monika shook her head. "I'd say it was because he wanted to take over the group. He needed to be the big cheese. We should call Philadelphia. See if the police staking out his house came up with anything."

Hayden threw down the cigarette. "Yeah. No use wasting more time here."

They were just about to get into his car to return to the hotel when Sheriff Billings pulled up beside them. "I thought you'd be here." Neither she nor Hayden answered. "I just got a report of a car being stolen from the Bailey farm just outside town. Old Man Bailey never uses it so he didn't notice until this morning."

Monika turned to Hayden before addressing the local lawman once more. "Did it have gas in it?"

"He kept a full tank in case of emergencies."

"Dasch could have made it all the way back to his house in Conshohocken," Monika asserted. She brought her fist down on the car.

"Let's get back there," Hayden said.

They both thanked the sheriff and got into the car. Monika knew the manhunt was only just beginning. Hayden told the head of the FBI task force they were leaving and drove back into Altoona. Monika suggested driving straight to Philadelphia, but Hayden insisted they pick up their things, including the car Monika had driven across the state. She gave him Dasch's address and arranged to meet him at the Nazi spy's house in just under four hours. Monika relived every conversation she'd had with Dasch on the highway east. Everything he'd referred to was to happen soon. It seemed he was just about to act. But what could he achieve alone? Bombing a ship in the port would be close to impossible without the others to back him up. She thought of what she'd seen in his basement—the rifle he was making, and the folder with the news articles and the mysterious word "duchess" written on it. Perhaps the key to solving the puzzle of what Dasch would do next was already in her mind.

She arrived at Dasch's house at the end of the working day, just as the other employees of the mill he worked in were trudging home with bags slung over their shoulders. A police car was sitting outside. Hayden hadn't arrived yet, but Monika was in no mood to wait. She parked beside the house and got out. Two police officers were sitting reading the newspaper.

"Can we help you, Girlie?" one man said as Monika knocked on the window.

"I'm part of the task force assigned to find Ernest Dasch. Have you seen him? How long have you been here?"

The policeman, a red-faced man with a red mustache, replied with a smile.

"Task force?" He turned to the officer beside him who

seemed to find it just as funny as he did. "The feds sent you, did they?"

The other policeman chimed in. "Sent you on a vital mission to clean the house?"

Monika ignored their comments.

"I tracked Ernest Dasch from Western Pennsylvania but have reason to believe he fled back here—"

"The red-faced officer with the red mustache interrupted her. "Wait just one minute here. Are you a kraut, too?" His smile melted. "Are you with this guy?"

Monika stood away from the window for a few seconds, trying to summon the patience not to punch this man in the face. She had no credentials to show him, and Hayden wouldn't have mentioned her on the phone.

"Have you seen any sign of Dasch?" she asked.

"Who are you, exactly, Girlie? If you're his girlfriend or something...."

Monika walked away from the car to wait for Hayden. She walked to the front of the house and stared at it, looking for any sign that the Nazi spy had come back.

The ten minutes it took for Hayden to arrive seemed more like hours. Monika jogged over to his car as he pulled up. "They wouldn't tell me anything," she said.

Hayden apologized on their behalf and walked over to the police car with her. He flashed a government ID to men. "She's with me."

Monika posed the question again. "So, have you seen him?"

The original police officer shook his head. "We haven't seen a thing. Feel free to take over if you want."

He and the other man chuckled to each other. Monika walked away, bristling with frustration. Hayden joined her on the sidewalk, out of earshot of the cops. "We missed him!" she hissed.

"We don't know that."

"He got out of Altoona and drove straight back here. God only knows where he might be now."

Hayden made an argument she didn't think he truly believed. "He could be dead at the bottom of that river for all we know."

"Do you really think that?"

He answered her question with a steely stare. "We need to get inside that house," he said after a few seconds.

Monika glanced over at the police car. The cops weren't paying them any attention. "And we can't hang around to get a warrant."

"You're really convinced he's planning something, aren't you? You ever consider he might have been trying to impress you?"

"I saw the look in his eyes. He wasn't flirting, I can assure you. We need to know if he was in that house."

"All right, but if we're to get in there without a warrant, we need our friends over yonder to take their leave as soon as possible."

"Leave that to me," Monika said and strolled over to the car. She wasn't sure how good she was looking after what she'd been through in the previous 48 hours, but her looks were something she'd always been able to rely on, and she was sure they wouldn't let her down now. The cops looked up as she approached them with a beaming smile. "Do you boys want a break? My boss told me he'd watch the house for an hour or so if you wanted to get something to eat or a cup of coffee."

The policemen turned to each other. "That'd be great," the first cop said.

"I don't think our man's coming back now, anyway," she explained. "But we'll keep an eye out for a little while longer, just in case."

"And this guy's a kraut?" the red-faced cop said. "He a friend of yours?"

"We'll see you in an hour or so, guys. After that, we should be able to call off the stakeout."

The policemen drove off with wide smiles on their faces.

"I can get us into the house," she said to Hayden.

"You did it before," he responded.

They walked around the back together, and she reached into her pocket for the lock picks. With the experience of the last time fresh in her mind, getting into the house proved easier than the previous time.

"Good work," Hayden said as she pushed the door open.

Monika didn't respond. The house was as quiet as it had been the first time she'd broken in, but not as clean. The cutting board was out, and the residue of the spam he'd cut on it was still visible.

"He was here," she asserted.

With no pressing need to check the rest of the house, Monika continued to the basement. Hayden stood beside her as she picked the lock. They walked down together. She flicked on the light. Her eyes were drawn first to the Nazi flag and then to the workbench. It was clean. The rifle he'd been working on was gone.

Monika turned to Hayden. "Dasch was making a rifle down here. He must have come back for it."

"Why would he risk coming back for a rifle?"

"If he intended to use it. And who knows what else he took? Maybe he had a stash of money upstairs."

Monika walked over to the desk. Hayden examined the news articles on the wall detailing Nazi victories in Europe. She was more interested in the fact that the manila folder she'd seen here last time was gone.

"Something else is missing," she said and began to search for the folder.

"What is it?" Hayden asked as she searched under the desk and through the boxes in the corner.

"A folder I found. It was full of old newspaper clippings, mainly about Roosevelt. It was like Dasch was compiling a dossier about him."

"He's obsessed. Was there any clue about what he was planning to do? Anything you forgot to mention that being here might make you remember?"

"There was a list of Roosevelt's speaking engagements and a word written on the outside of the folder—duchess."

"As in Dutchess County?"

"I have no idea."

"It's in upstate New York. You think Dasch might be planning on taking a shot at the President in Dutchess County? That's where his ancestral home is. He was born there."

"It doesn't seem like an easy place to try to assassinate the President. Surely the security there would be second only to the White House itself. It must be crawling with Secret Service agents."

Hayden looked around before bringing his eyes back to hers. "I don't know much about the security up there, but I can find out. Is that what you garnered from searching here, that Dasch was going to try to shoot the President in Dutchess County? I can't imagine Roosevelt is up there too much at the moment with the war raging. He's going to be in Philly in two days, making a speech outside Independence Hall."

"How is Dutchess County spelled? With or without a t?"

"With as far as I remember."

"The word I saw written down was "duchess" without a t."

"That's an easy mistake to make, especially since English isn't Dasch's first language."

Monika walked over to the corner to search behind the boxes. "What if it wasn't a mistake?" she said and turned back to him.

"Listen, we don't know what this guy is up to. I'm pretty sure he's alive now, but if I were him, I'd run for the hills."

She shook her head. "He wants to make a splash—to do something to change the face of the war. What else could that be other than assassinating Roosevelt?"

"I don't know. The chance of getting near the President must be thousands to one, particularly on his estate in Dutchess County, but I'll make some calls and have them double the security up there until we catch Dasch."

They resumed the search but found little else of interest. Dasch had come through the house, taken his folder and his rifle, eaten something, and packed a suitcase of clothes.

"What next?" Monika asked as they stepped out of the house. The police car still hadn't returned. There seemed little need for them now.

"I make a call to the Secret Service and tell them we think there's an elevated threat."

"Then we go to the mill where Dasch works and find out if any of his friends there knew anything about his plans."

Hayden took a cigarette from his pocket and lit it as they walked back to the car. "Don't forget about Burger. He might be willing to make a deal to save his skin. He's facing the electric chair."

"Where is he?"

"On his way to D.C. I'm going down there tomorrow morning to interrogate him."

"I don't think he knows anything, and he'll tell you Dasch personally sank the Titanic to save himself, but by all means, give it a try."

"So, I have your permission, do I?" Hayden said and looked at her.

Monika ignored what he said. "It doesn't feel right to me. Attacking Roosevelt's home at some far-off date when the President returns there doesn't fit with what Dasch said. Everything he told me led me to believe that he was planning something soon."

"And what fits the definition of soon?"

"The President's speech outside Independence Hall in two days. Maybe that's what he was building the rifle for. It might have a special scope or an engineered barrel to fire from long distance."

"I'll pass on your concerns to the Secret Service. Those guys don't take chances. In the meantime, come down to D.C. with me, and we'll see what we can get from the other men. I'll get you the gas you need, and if you want to come back up to Philly for the President's speech on Friday, you do that."

Leaving didn't feel right, but Hayden's logic was hard to argue with. They waited a few minutes for the cops to come back and then dismissed them.

It was a short drive to the steel mill. They parked on the street outside and walked together into the plant. The heat of molten metal struck her as they walked up. The sound of metal clanking and machinery whirring made talking difficult, and they had to shout to make themselves heard. Hayden asked the first worker they saw where they could find the foreman. He pointed a finger toward a prefabricated office in the corner. Hayden thanked the man, and they walked over.

Hayden knocked and opened the door without waiting for a response. The foreman, a large man with a mustache and a receding hairline, was sitting behind the desk shuffling through some papers as they walked in. His protective mask was folded up over his head. His cheeks were still flushed red from the heat of the molten metal. The suspicious look on his face disappeared when Hayden flashed his government credentials.

"Tobias Lindmerth," the foreman said and shook Hayden's hand. Monika greeted him the same way, and they sat in front of his desk.

"We're here to ask about Ernest Dasch," Hayden began. Monika understood that it was best if he did the talking.

"You know where he is? He was supposed to be back in work today."

"He's a person of interest in our investigation. If, by some remote chance, he does happen to come back, please call the police as soon as possible."

Tobias shook his head. "What did he do?"

"Is it a surprise to you that we're looking for him?"

The foreman picked up a pencil between his fingers and twirled it back and forth. "No. He was a good worker but kept to himself. Didn't have any friends in here. I always thought he was a little shifty. And, of course, the fact is that he's a kraut. You can't trust 'em, can you?"

Monika shook her head but kept her mouth shut.

Hayden continued. "Is there anyone in here that might know where he is, or if he wanted to get away, who he'd run to?"

"I don't think I recall seeing him chatting to anyone here in any way that might suggest they'd be close. A lot of the guys go out on Friday nights, but he never came along—not one time in all the years he worked here."

"Did he ever talk about any anti-government sentiment? Or mention the president?"

"Not that I heard about. But he'd have some nerve doing that around here with that accent of his. He'd know better than to talk like that in front of these men."

Hayden stood up and shook Lindmerth's hand again. "Thanks for your time."

"What'd he do, anyway?"

"Keep an eye on the papers. You'll find out soon enough."

Talking to a few more of the men confirmed what the foreman had said, and as Monika thought, they left none the wiser as to what Dasch's plans were. Questioning his neighbors seemed pointless and would be a job better left to the local police, anyway.

Their next stop was a local hotel, where Hayden made the

phone calls to the Secret Service and the local police in Conshohocken. Monika stood beside him, listening in as he told them what he knew. After a few minutes, he hung up the phone and turned to her.

"My contact in the Secret Service said they'll be extra vigilant at the President's next few events, but I don't know what that means coming from them. It's their business to be paranoid. The local cops are going to maintain surveillance on his house in case he shows up again."

"He's not going back there again."

"I know that, and you know that, but they're insisting. They're going to talk to his neighbors, too, just in case."

"Waste of time," Monika said.

Hayden crossed his arms. "What do you suggest?"

Her words were succinct and sharp. "We put his description in the papers. Do a press conference. Get the public working for us. He's out there somewhere. Someone's seen him or the car he stole in Altoona."

Hayden's face tightened. "The powers that be don't want to publicize this until we have every Nazi spy in custody."

"What?"

"Put yourself in their place, Ritter. How's it going to look if the papers cover this? Can you imagine the panic if the American people knew there was a Nazi spy on the loose? That's what their superiors in the Abwehr are aiming for—to break the will of the people to fight. We have to seem like we have the situation in hand."

"Even if we don't?"

"Even if we don't. It's up to us to find this man. And we'll do it. The other saboteurs will lead us to him. I'm sure they know something, even if they don't think they do."

"So the PR battle is more important than the President's life?"

Hayden laughed and shook his head. "This is politics, Ritter. You didn't know you were a politician now?"

"It wasn't what I signed up for, sir."

"But it's the job. For now, at least."

Monika tried to let her frustrations go. Hayden's point wasn't hard to understand but she didn't agree with it. They drove back into the city. She still had thousands of dollars left from the money she'd been given before landing in Florida and treated them to separate five-star rooms and dinner. Monika lay in bed for hours, going over every little thing Dasch said to her, searching for clues in every syllable. But she found none. Tomorrow would be telling.

14

The more she thought about it, the more convinced she became that Roosevelt himself was Dasch's target, but where, when, and how? Getting to the President was a difficult task for a trained team like the one they'd just arrested. Doing it alone would require equal parts luck and skill. Dasch would need something close to a miracle to kill FDR, but perhaps just a public attempt by a German spy on the run would be a victory in and of itself. It would represent a major PR coup for Hitler and might shake the American will to fight just when it mattered most.

Monika wondered if Roosevelt knew about the possible threat to his life but doubted he'd been told. He likely received dozens of such warnings a week. The fact was she was operating on a hunch, and, as Hayden had reminded her, she had no direct evidence of Dasch's plot.

Hayden parked on a city street that looked like any other and brought her inside a building that she would have thought was a lawyers' office. The only difference was the soldier who greeted them at the door.

The guard who'd met them at the door passed them off to

another soldier, who took them downstairs to a heavy basement door. He opened it with a key he took from his belt and led them into a hallway with another guard sitting reading a newspaper.

"The interrogation room is the door at the end," the first soldier said. He handed Hayden the keys. "You want me to come in with you?"

"I think it'll be good for you to stay outside," Hayden responded. "We'll call you if we need you."

The soldier eyed Monika as if he couldn't believe Hayden was bringing her in with him but didn't verbalize his thoughts.

"Who are you here to see?"

"George Burger," Monika said.

She and Hayden had agreed to interrogate Burger together.

The soldier nodded and walked them to the interrogation room where they sat down at the single gray table in the middle of the dank room, lit only by two lightbulbs hanging overhead.

Two minutes later, the guard brought in Burger. His jawline tightened as he saw Monika.

"What are you doing here?" he asked in German.

"I'm here to help you, George," she said calmly. "Take a seat."

The youthful Nazi spy was in handcuffs. He held up his wrists to the guard. "Can you take them off just for the interview?" The soldier shook his head and walked out. Burger dropped into the chair opposite Monika and Hayden.

"Help me?" he said. "That's a laugh. When did the Americans get to you? How much was selling out the Fatherland worth?"

Hayden leaned forward and clasped his hands over the table. He spoke in fluent German. "You're looking at the death penalty for treason, George. How old are you? 22?"

Burger's lips tightened. The fear he was trying to hide was plain to see on his face. He leaned forward. "I was set up. I had no idea what we were doing." He pointed at Monika. "This woman entrapped me!"

"Let us help you," Hayden said. "Tell us what we need to know, and you might just survive this."

"What you want to know?" he replied. "What might that be?"

Hayden hesitated for a few seconds before continuing. "We killed all your colleagues, except.... except perhaps for one man."

"Let me guess—Dasch?" Burger said. "That man is more slippery than a greased-up eel."

"How well do you know him?" Monika asked.

Burger hesitated, as if weighing the truth against what could get him out of this situation. "Dasch is a hard man to know."

"He was the one who planned the previous operations, wasn't he? Did he share the process of how he came up with them?" she asked.

Burger shook his head. "We met up, and he went through the missions step by step. It wasn't a democratic process, so to speak."

Hayden interjected. "Did you train with him in Germany?"

"No."

Hayden reached into his pocket for a pack of cigarettes. He offered one to Burger, who accepted. The OSS man lit the Nazi spy's cigarette before his own. Soon, the air was thick with gray, swirling smoke.

"Did Dasch mention any dreams he had of striking a decisive blow against the American Government?"

Burger affirmed what Monika had said. "Regularly. But he wasn't any different than the rest of us. We all talked about that. It might have been the most common conversation we had."

"Did he ever mention anything specific? Any future missions he was planning?"

"Not to me."

"Did he have a girlfriend?" Hayden asked.

"Not that I know of. He wasn't one to share details of his personal life. He didn't go out with the rest of us much."

Frustration coursed through Monika's system. "Do you know of anywhere he might go to hide away for a while?" Burger shook his head.

"You're not giving us much here, George," Hayden reminded him. "Don't forget your life depends on this."

The boy was pale, and his skin was clammy. "You don't think I know that?" he shouted. "I don't know. If I did, I'd tell you. I'm not a madman, I don't want to die."

"What about Dasch?" Hayden asked.

"What do you mean?"

"Is he a madman?"

"If you're asking what he'll do to further the cause—the answer is anything. He never seemed to have any thoughts outside the missions. He never mentioned any hobbies, or even people he knew. He spoke about his work sometimes, but he showed little interest in it. It was just a way to sustain himself. The other men were dedicated to the cause, but he was different. He didn't seem to have anything else in his life apart from serving the Führer."

"Apart from his organizational abilities, does Dasch have any special skills we don't know about?" Hayden asked.

Burgers shot back the words. "He was the best of us with weapons. He and Thiel made the bombs we used in Baltimore and the other missions. Once, I heard him mention his prowess with making guns."

"Did he ever talk about building a special sniper rifle?" Monika asked.

"Never. Every time he started talking, he seemed to hold himself back. Even with us," Burger explained.

"What about the word 'Duchess?' Does that mean anything to you?"

His face contorted in confusion. "What? I have no idea what you're talking about."

Disappointed, Monika sat forward. "I spoke to Dasch several times, but never in a casual, social manner. Did you ever spend time with him when he relaxed?"

"He didn't relax much."

"Did he ever make jokes?" she asked.

"He did enjoy joining in on certain jokes. The ones we made about blowing up the Statue of Liberty or filling the Grand Canyon with cement."

"Do you remember any specific jokes he made?"

Burger sat back in his seat and stared past them as if trying to search his memories. "He's not exactly Bob Hope, but I think I can remember some things he said."

"Such as?" Monika inquired.

"We all made jokes about blowing up the White House, but he mentioned shooting Roosevelt. It wasn't as funny as the other gags, but we kept going."

Monika peered across at Hayden. "I don't suppose he has the gift," she continued.

Burger held up his hands. "I don't know much else. But if I can help in any way...."

Hayden stubbed out his cigarette. "How about telling us everything you know about the training mechanism in Germany?"

Burger closed his eyes for a moment before nodding his approval.

"That's the right decision, George. One that might just save your life," Hayden said.

The chair screeched on the floor as Monika stood up. She didn't make eye contact with the young Nazi agent as she and

Hayden left the room. The soldier nodded to them as he opened the door.

"Who do you need to see next?" he said.

"Just give us a moment, please," Monika responded.

The guard did as he was told and walked down to the other man, who was still in his chair reading the newspaper.

"We've got to get to Philadelphia before the President's speech tomorrow," she whispered with as much intensity as she could muster.

The OSS man seemed frustrated with her. "I've already warned the Secret Service. They'll be on the lookout. The best thing we can do is to stay here and interrogate these men together. We have no idea what we can still get out of them."

"Do you think we can get them to call off the appearance? I didn't think FDR had these outdoor public events in him anymore. He'd probably jump at the chance to skip it."

"If he could jump," Hayden murmured. "Apparently, he's feeling better and thought a speech in front of Independence Hall would galvanize the war effort. I can't convince them to cancel the event based on what we have. The President receives dozens of death threats a week. We have no evidence that this is any more serious than any of the others."

"Dasch is a highly motivated man, intent on creating as much havoc as possible. The one thing I do know he talked about was doing something huge to disrupt the course of the entire war! What better way than to assassinate the President? It could destroy the will of the American people to fight and leave the British and the Soviets high and dry."

"We've been over this, Ritter, but I'll tell you what: How about we head up to Philadelphia later this evening? We can keep an eye on the situation there ourselves and hopefully get to see the President make a nice, uneventful speech. That's the best I can do."

"You're underestimating how dangerous Dasch is."

"I'm working with the facts we have, but I'll meet you halfway. We'll go to Philly. Deal?" He held out his hand.

"Deal," she said and shook it.

She tried to push aside her anger and frustration. Hayden made a good point. She was operating almost entirely on instinct, but she trusted her gut. Her hunch would have to wait until the next day.

"What's going to happen to Burger?" Monika asked as they walked out onto the street. The day was succumbing to darkness, and streetlights were blinking on above their heads.

"Too early to say. He might prove valuable enough to avoid the chair."

They got into his car, parked directly outside on the street. Monika got in the passenger side.

"Are we leaving for Philly?"

"Not yet," he answered. He smiled at her scowl. "Let's get dinner first. Dasch isn't going to take a shot at Roosevelt tonight! The speech isn't until three o'clock tomorrow afternoon. We'll be there, I guarantee that."

Monika didn't agree with him, but he was her superior officer, and she kept her mouth shut. They had a meal in an Italian place Hayden knew. Pasta wasn't rationed, and she enjoyed a plate of rigatoni as Hayden talked about the politics of capturing the men.

"The job isn't done yet. We might have to squash the story if we don't catch Dasch soon," he said with a mouthful of penne.

"What about if Dasch assassinates the President? How will that look?"

Hayden didn't answer, instead preferring to fork another piece of penne into his mouth.

After dinner ended, they set off for Philadelphia, three hours away. The further they drove, the more conviction Monika had in her hunch. Dasch was desperate and alone now. She, and the rest of the intelligence community, had wondered at first how deep the Nazi network went. It was shallower than they'd feared. Doubtless, there were thousands, or possibly even hundreds of thousands of Nazi sympathizers in the US. The people who'd joined the German American Bund and who'd packed out Madison Square Garden a few short years before hadn't disappeared. They just weren't as forthright with their beliefs now. Perhaps some of them changed their minds when some of Hitler's atrocities began to come to light, but Monika was sure most of them either didn't believe the reports or care what they said. It seemed those who followed Hitler's teachings, be they in Michigan or Munich, did so for life. To them, he was the greatest leader in the history of the world and could do no wrong. Men like Dasch weren't for changing. He would be dead soon one way or the other. It would be up to her that he didn't die as one of the most notorious men in history.

15

Monika and Hayden arrived at Independence Hall at nine o'clock the next morning. Hayden showed his ID to one of the policemen manning the barricades that had been set up at the edge of Chestnut Steet and South 4th Street to cordon off the area. All four corners of the mall had been cordoned off. No crowds had gathered yet. The area was crawling with dozens of police and men in suits who Monika presumed were Secret Service. The cop, a young man with a red face, looked them up and down before passing their credentials back. Monika didn't have an ID to show she was an OSS agent, and hence was unarmed as she passed through the gates.

"Who's in charge?" Hayden asked.

"Captain Murphy," the man replied and pointed toward a uniformed officer with a mustache and an impressive beer belly standing about 30 feet away.

They walked past the red brick building where the Declaration of Independence had been adopted on a hot July day 167 years before. Monika scanned the park in front of the old buildings. Hundreds of seats had already been set up in rows of 20. Two trucks were unloading more. The mall was surrounded by buildings, some up to eight stories high. Monika searched for open windows or other places Dasch could shoot from. Everything was quiet. He'd have no reason to be in place this early. The speech wasn't for another five hours. The inclement weather Monika had been hoping for wasn't going to come. Clear skies and bright sunshine meant the ceremony to designate the mall as a new national park would go ahead as planned. This wasn't going to be easy. Monika was confident that Hayden was taking the threat seriously, but she seemed to be the only one who appreciated exactly who Dasch was. She couldn't imagine a more dangerous man.

The police captain was standing with two men in suits. One of them was holding a metal contraption Monika had seen during training. It was a new invention known as a "handie talkie," and was like a portable telephone in your hand. Seeing the Secret Service utilizing such a new technology was comforting. Hayden approached the men first. It was the way it had to be. He was her superior officer.

"Captain Murphy?" Hayden said as they reached the small group of men. They seemed to be having a casual conversation about the state of the war.

The police captain whirled around. He smiled as he saw Monika. She did her best not to cringe. The other two men, both clean-shaven and in their late 20s looked her up and down in a different but similarly objectionable manner.

"What can I do for you?" Murphy said.

"Bill Hayden." He shook the captain's hand. "We spoke on the phone yesterday?" Murphy looked puzzled. "About the threat to the President?"

"Oh, yes. I remember now. This is Arnold Swain, and Thomas Gardener of the Secret Service." Both men shook Hayden's hand while ignoring Monika.

"This is Agent Ritter," the OSS man said. "She's the one who sniffed out the potential problem."

"A girl, eh?" Captain Murphy laughed. "All very modern, isn't it?" he said to the other three men.

Monika ignored him. "I infiltrated a circle of German spies. They are all dead or captured... except for one man—Ernest Dasch. In my opinion, he's the most dangerous of them all. And I have reason to believe he is planning an attempt on the President's life today."

Swain, a handsome man with a chiselled face and blond hair, was first to speak. "What makes you think that? Seems like a tough assignment."

"He said he wanted to do something huge that might subvert the direction of the war. And we found rifle-making equipment and a list of the President's upcoming events in his basement."

"Doesn't sound like much," Murphy replied. "He could be a hunter with an interest in politics."

"The man is a trained assassin," she snapped. "He's on his own now, with nothing to lose. Can we alert your agents to the threat?"

Swain nodded. "Do you have a description for him?"

"We do," Hayden said and reached into his pocket for the factsheet they'd written up about Dasch the night before.

Swain took a few seconds to read over it before handing it to his colleague. "I'll call my men back for a meeting in a few minutes. They're not all in position yet."

"How many agents do you have here today?"

Swain pointed up at the buildings that overlooked the mall. "We'll have snipers on each of the rooftops overlooking the crowd and someone at the door of each building. The police are blocking off the entrance and searching everyone who comes in. The crowd inside the barriers is by invitation only, but we'll still have men among them. We'll have agents beside and in front of where the President speaks."

"What about access to the buildings overlooking the mall?"

"We'll go through them looking for your man with the help of the local police," Swain asserted. Murphy looked a little nonplussed, but the Secret Service man didn't seem to care. "How skilled a shooter is this man?"

"An Abwehr trained marksman. Highly proficient," she answered.

"Where would the best shooting positions be?" Hayden asked.

Swain turned around to face the buildings. "Apart from the crowd right here in front? I'd say in any of the higher floors in the buildings along the sides. If I couldn't get in to sit with the rest of the dignitaries, that's where I'd be. Ideal shooting positions would be approximately five stories above the President's location. They'll have to wait until he takes the podium, several lines into his speech. That way he'll be completely static, at his most exposed. The shot will require a large caliber weapon— not the type of thing that'd be easy to smuggle around the streets on a day like today when the place is crawling with cops and Secret Service."

"So, that means the rifle would most likely already be in place," Monika added.

"If that's the way he intends to take the shot," Swain said. "The easiest way would be from a few feet away around where we're standing." He turned around to the podium where the lectern was being set up. It was about 15 feet away. There'll be agents stationed in front. If he managed to get in somehow, he could shoot from the crowd with a small arm. If he's as good as you say he is, he could score a hit."

Thomas Gardener, the man holding the handie talkie spoke up for the first time. "But we're going to make sure that can't happen. We'll have you down here at the front to keep an eye out for Dasch. You've seen him with your own eyes?"

"I've spoken to him. Almost killed him the other day," she answered.

The men laughed. Her ribs ached as she joined in.

"You can be our eyes on the ground. A description is useful, but if he's wearing an effective disguise, our men might not be able to recognize him as you would."

"I'm here and available to check the crowd as they come in," Monika said.

"Excellent," Gardener answered.

Murphy had been standing listening during the entire conversation but hadn't said a word.

"Can you get the description to the local police?" Monika asked him.

He took one of the printed sheets she handed him and looked over it for a few seconds. "I'll make sure they know. How likely is this?"

Monika looked at Hayden. "We think it's a distinct possibility, but better safe than sorry."

The police captain grunted a few incomprehensible words under his breath before walking away.

Gardener brought the talkie to his ear and called the agents in the vicinity for a meeting. "We have word of a viable threat," he said.

A few minutes later, 15 agents, some in suits, others in black sniper's clothing, gathered around. The sound of workmen building the podium in the background punctuated Swain's sentences as he explained the situation. Monika wondered if the police were receiving the same briefing from Murphy. She doubted it.

Monika tried to remember the details from her search of Dasch's house. She tried to remember every word he'd ever said to her and every nuance and facial expression he'd exhibited while talking. She came up with nothing.

"Can I go along with one of the snipers when they leave, and get a panoramic view of the mall?" Monika asked when Swain had finished.

"Sure," the Secret Service agent agreed. "Wicker, can you take Miss Ritter along with you? Just to give her a view of the area."

The sniper nodded. "Yes, sir."

Wicker was a man in his mid-20s with muscular forearms and an M1903A4 rifle on his back.

"You like the rifle?" she asked Wicker as they walked away.

"I do. You ever use it?" he asked facetiously.

"The scope is good, but the action sticks and curtails any ideas you might have about rapid fire. I never had any problems with the bolt coming apart, but I've seen it happen."

"Yeah, too many times," he replied, his eyebrows raised.

He led her up to one of the red brick buildings overlooking the mall. She walked up the steps behind him. Wicker explained who she was to the two officers on duty, and they proceeded inside.

"What is this place? The Bourse?" she asked.

"It's a commodities exchange," Wicker answered. "The fat cats have a day off today. I'm sure we'll see a bunch of them sitting out on the lawn later for the speech."

She followed him into the elevator, where an operator brought them up to an office on the ninth floor. A ladder behind a door that said, 'restricted access,' brought them up to the roof.

"This is my position," Wicker said and lay down on his belly by the edge of the building.

"May I?" Monika gestured to the rifle.

"By all means."

She got down beside him and scanned the area through the

rifle scope. The stage was about four hundred yards away—well within range of his powerful weapon. The chairs were almost fully laid out. Workers were buzzing around the mall getting the final preparations in place for the President's arrival. Nothing seemed out of the ordinary.

"Where are you, Dasch?" she whispered to herself as she ran the scope over the buildings opposite.

"It's as much my job to focus on the buildings themselves as the crowd. If I see a window open, I'll zero in on it in seconds," Wicker told her.

"I think he's more likely to fire from a distance than up close. Dasch didn't seem like the type who'd willingly martyr himself. He'll want to slip away when the deed is done."

"No one's getting to the President. Not on my watch," Wicker answered.

Monika spent another few minutes examining the area through the sight. There didn't seem any obvious place for Dasch to shoot from. The doors to all the buildings were guarded. Unless he was already holed up in a room overlooking the mall, she couldn't see a way. And if he did manage to gain access to somewhere, Wicker and his buddies would take him out before he could get a round off.

Monika pushed herself off the surface of the roof and wished Wicker luck.

"Hey, maybe I'll see you after this for a drink?" the sniper asked.

"I'm married," she said and walked away.

"Had to try," she heard him say as she reached the door.

Hayden was by the stage when Monika found him a few minutes later. They took a walk around the mall. She was comforted by the fact that they were stopped several times as they strolled around, but wondered if Dasch had a fake ID he could flash to fool the Secret Service and police. It was impossible to know, but that didn't stop the thought from swirling around in her head.

As she approached Hayden, the word "Duchess" appeared in her mind. Perhaps it had been referring to the county Roosevelt lived in, but why would Dasch write it down? It didn't make sense.

Monika didn't raise her concerns about that word she'd seen written on the folder in Dasch's house to her boss, she just apprised him of what she'd learned from her trip to the roof of the Bourse building.

Hayden nodded. "It seems the Secret Service men have everything in hand, but we'll stay to help out."

People were already filing into the mall from the side streets perpendicular to the mall. It was a fine day so several of the men in suits came in with their jackets draped across their arms. The ladies were decked out in dresses that seemed out of place during times like these. Monika stood beside two policemen, checking each person's face they let through.

The President's limousine arrived 30 minutes before he was set to take the stage. The Governor of Pennsylvania, Arthur James, was already on stage, urging the crowd to buy the precious war bonds that would fuel the Allied victory overseas. A massive American flag was pinned to a wall erected behind the platform the lectern was on, and a dozen soldiers and sailors stood to attention on either side of the governor. The crowd clapped at the appropriate times and sometimes even cheered, but there was no doubt who the main attraction was.

Monika was standing on the corner of Chestnut Street and South 5th Street, to the left of the stage. The crowd was largely in their seats now, with just a few stragglers still coming through the gates to proffer their invitations to the on-duty policemen. Monika had examined every person's face who'd walked through and was confident Hayden had done the same thing at the other corner. She peered out at the crowd watching the governor speak, searching for Dasch's face. Doubts began to enter her mind, and she knew if she was no longer sure, Hayden, Swain, and the others had probably given up on Dasch showing his face long ago. Monika walked along the side, still staring at the people watching. She shook her head and walked back to where she'd been. Hundreds of people were gathered at the barricades, and even though smuggling a rifle among the other passers-by who'd stopped to watch would be almost impossible, she examined them. A dozen police officers stood watching them. It seemed that attacking Roosevelt's home in Dutchess County might have been an easier target.

Monika made her way back to her corner. Hayden was standing on the opposite side of the stage. He waved across to her as Governor James finished his speech. She stood still as he shuffled across to where she was standing.

"Doesn't look like our man is showing today," he said as he arrived beside her. "Good work, anyway," he continued. "We'll take a trip to his house in New York next week and try to find out when the President might be in residence."

Monika didn't answer. The crowd stood as President Roosevelt took the stage. A sharp feeling in Monika's chest stopped her from clapping along with everyone else. The time to take the shot was coming up. Swain and Gardener stood on each side of President Roosevelt, who waved to the crowd before approaching the stage. The President looked frail and hunched over to lean on the heavy wooden lectern. He stood to attention with the rest of the crowd as the band on the far side began to play The Star-Spangled Banner. Hayden stood with his hand on his chest, singing along with the crowd. Monika scanned the buildings and the crowd around the mall. She saw Wicker's rifle protruding off the edge of the Bourse, but nothing else.

The anthem ended, the crowd took their seats once more, and the President began to speak.

"I stand before you today during one of the great moments in the history of our nation. The past year was perhaps the most crucial of our lives for modern civilization. The coming year will be filled with violent conflicts—yet with the high promise of better things. I have been inspired by the great qualities of our fighting men. They have demonstrated these qualities in adversity as well as victory. As long as our flag flies over the Capitol, Americans will honor the soldiers, sailors, and marines who fought our first battles of this war against overwhelming odds, the heroes, living and dead, of Wake and Bataan and Guadalcanal, of the Java Sea and Midway and the North Atlantic convoys. Their unconquerable spirit will live forever."

The people in the crowd rose to their feet to applaud. President Roosevelt stood back to accept their acclaim for a few seconds.

A voice from behind her caused Monika to turn around. A man and his wife were at the barricades 20 feet behind where she was standing. The two policemen still on duty there had stopped them. An instinct Monika couldn't explain drove her to walk back to them. Hayden hesitated at first but then followed her.

The man, who looked to be in his early 30s, was arguing with the officers on duty. His wife was standing behind him, with her arms folded in disgust.

"I know we're late," he said. "But please, we've been looking forward to this for months."

No disguise could have made Dasch look like him. The man was several inches smaller with a completely different shaped face.

"I can't let you in. Not now," one of the cops said. "This is the best I can do for you."

"We can hardly see!" the man said.

His wife unfolded her arms, but the disgruntled look on her

face remained the same. "We should have stayed at home, Gerry," she said. "We'd get a better view from our apartment."

Monika stepped forward. "Where is that?"

"Where is what?" the woman said.

"Your apartment?"

She turned and pointed to a building just behind them on Chestnut Street, outside the barricaded area. "Right there," she said. "The Duchess Apartments."

Monika's stomach dropped. "The Duchess Apartments? Duchess?"

"Yeah, we can get a perfect view if we lean out the window a little."

Monika looked at Hayden, but the OSS man was already pushing past the policemen.

"Where are you going?" one of the cops asked.

Hayden pulled his ID and they let him and Monika through. The building was two hundred yards up the street on the right-hand side and afforded an unobstructed view of the side of the President's platform. Monika cursed herself for being so stupid. She pushed past pedestrians gathered on the sidewalk to get a glimpse of President Roosevelt. He was stationary, and several paragraphs into his speech. This was the time to take the shot. The apartment block, a new-looking building with long windows shining in the sun, was 50 yards away when she saw the window open on the third floor. The sound of the President's voice echoed through the Tannoy system in the mall.

"Hayden!" she screamed. The barrel of a rifle pushed through the opening.

The OSS man drew his pistol from a holster under his armpit. He fell to one knee and fired. The bullets smashed the glass. The crowd on the street around them screamed and scattered. Police came running. The sound of the President's voice stopped. Monika caught a glimpse of Dasch. He was unhurt and brought the rifle to bear on Hayden and fired. The bullet struck Hayden in the upper chest. His gun fell to the ground. Monika rushed to him.

"I'm okay," he spluttered. "Go get Dasch."

She picked up Hayden's gun and ran into the apartment building. Screaming civilians pushed past her as they fled through the front door.

"Government business," she shouted. "Stand aside!"

She found space to run up the stairwell. Dasch wouldn't hang around now. The assassination attempt was over. Roosevelt had already been bundled off the stage by the Secret Service and was probably in the car already. She took no pleasure in foiling the attempt on the President's life. Not yet. It was only a matter of time until Dasch tried something as audacious as this again. She'd only be satisfied once he was neutralized. Dead or alive didn't matter.

Monika reached the second floor and kept running. Looking up, she caught a glimpse of Dasch two floors above her. She took aim and fired but struck the banister. He peered down and pointed a handgun at her. She dodged the shot and kept running. Her lungs were burning as she reached a door at the top of the stairs on the fourth floor. It was ajar and marked "Roof Access."

Monika used the barrel of the pistol to push it open. Three shots rang out as soon as it moved and the metal door flew back in her face. Without hesitating, she pushed it open again and jumped through, rolling away from the bullets colliding with the door frame. She found a wide chimney pit to take cover behind. Another bullet zipped over her head. She peered up a few seconds later and saw Dasch running, his rifle slung over his shoulder. The sound of police sirens came from the street below, but she was sure Dasch had already figured an escape route. She leaped off the gravel that covered the roof and began to chase after him. He was twenty yards ahead and running toward the gap between the Duchess Apartments and the building next to it. He turned to fire, but Monika was ready and let a shot go before he could. It missed, and he turned to continue sprinting toward the gap. Without dropping his pace Dasch leaped off the edge of the building and landed on the next. He rose to his feet and kept running. The chasm was about six feet wide, but the fall was four stories. Monika jumped across, landed on her feet and kept running.

Dasch ducked behind a wall and turned to fire at her. Monika had only two bullets left in her gun. The Nazi spy fired at her and then turned to run again. She took careful aim and fired. The bullet struck Dasch just above his right hip. He called out in pain and fell to his haunches. The rifle slid off his shoulder. He discarded it and raised himself to his feet again. He was 15 yards from Monika, but she had only one bullet left. If she missed, she was probably dead. Blood poured down Dasch's leg, but somehow, he began running again, albeit not at the same speed as before. He turned to fire at her again but the shot was wild and went nowhere near her. She ran after him, gaining with every step as he neared the edge of the building. This was probably all part of his plan to escape. The police were likely only storming the Duchess Apartments. If he could reach the street through the next building, he could still escape.

Monika was five yards behind him as he jumped across the gap to the next building, but his injured hip curtailed the leap, and he fell a foot short. He grasped onto the ledge of the next building as Monika reached him.

She pointed the gun. "It's over, Dasch."

He huffed and puffed as he struggled to pull himself up over the edge. "Help me!" he gasped.

She noted that his pistol was tucked in his belt. Monika took a few steps back and ran to leap over to the next rooftop.

Putting down the gun beside her, she got down on her knees above him and reached down. She looked directly into his eyes and saw the pain burning through them. "Take my hand."

Dasch reached up to her with his right hand. Monika took it with both hands and heaved backward bringing his weight up. Dasch placed his right elbow on the ledge as she let go. But then she saw the look in his eyes change. His legs still dangling off the edge, he reached for the gun in his belt. He brought it up as she lunged for her pistol. Dasch leveled his gun at her just as she pulled the trigger. The shot hit him in the face, and he tumbled backward, clutching at thin air just as he had above that river at Horseshoe Curve. But this time there was no water to break his fall. His body plummeted down and collided with the pavement below with a sickening thud. Monika fell on her stomach and stared over the edge of the building. Dasch's unmoving corpse was lying beside a dumpster in the alley below. A small crowd of onlookers gathered around it.

Monika pulled back from the edge of the building and lay on her back to stare up at the blue sky above. It took her a few seconds to regain her breath. She stood up and walked over to the door from the roof which would lead her downstairs.

Hayden was in the back of an ambulance as she arrived back where she'd started, outside the Duchess Apartments. The window from which Dasch had tried to shoot the President from was caved in—a black morass among the others. Monika pushed past the police officers on the sidewalk and stepped into the back of the ambulance.

Hayden grimaced in pain as he sat up. "Where's Dasch?"

"In the alley about three hundred yards away. He's dead." She took his hand. "How about you?"

"I'll be fine," he coughed. "Not the first time a German shot me."

"I won't take that personally."

"Nor should you. Good work, Ritter. You were right." He nodded at her. "You got my gun?"

"No bullets left now, though."

"We need to get your friend to the hospital," one of the medics said.

Monika nodded and stepped back onto the sidewalk. She watched as the ambulance started down the street and blazed around the corner in a flurry of lights and noise.

16

Two weeks later.

Monika was 15 minutes early, but the soldier at the entrance let her through anyway. A man in a suit met her inside the door. He had a clipboard in his hand. She presented her ID and he led her inside to a waiting room. Monika picked up a newspaper and read through the headlines. American tanks had just defeated a force of Germans in Tunisia, but there was more than enough bad news to counter the good. German U-boats were inflicting devastating losses on Allied convoys in the North Atlantic. She threw the broadsheet back on the table and sat back. Thoughts of her parents drifted into her mind as she sat on the comfortable white couch. She tried to gauge how they'd react to this, but it was impossible. They'd never considered leaving Germany, let alone moving to America. Everything they knew about this country they'd read in books or seen in movies. As much as Monika hated to admit it to herself, the memories of her mother she was trying to cling to were fading. She could still envision her beautiful face, her kind smile, but her aura was dissipating. The feeling of being around her was foreign to Monika now. She had been 13 when her mother died—almost half her lifetime ago. It was hard to figure out how she'd react to the path Monika had taken. One thing she was sure of was how proud her mother and father both would have been as she sat in the waiting room outside the Oval Office for an audience with the President of the United States.

A young man about her age in a gray suit came to her.

"The President will see you now."

Monika stood up and nodded. She gulped back a deep breath in an attempt to calm her nerves and followed the aide toward a white door. He opened it for her. The President was sitting alone on a couch in the middle of the room. He stood to greet her as the aide showed her inside.

"Miss Ritter, I presume?" he said and walked toward her.

"Yes, Mr. President."

His hands were warm. He took her outstretched hand between his palms with a wide smile. "You're the person I owe my life to." He released her hand and gestured toward the couch. His movements were slow and labored. The aide helped him sit down.

"Sorry about that," he said. "I've been a little stiff lately."

Monika responded with a smile, waiting for him to begin.

"I brought you here today to thank you personally for what you did, not just for me, but for the war effort as a whole. I'm sure you know better than most what a PR coup assassinating me would have been for Hitler."

"I was just doing my duty, Mr. President."

"From what I hear, you went above and beyond that."

She couldn't help the smile that spread across her face. "Thank you, Mr. President."

"Call me Governor," he said. "It puts me at ease."

"Yes, Governor."

"Thank you for everything you did. The Allied Powers are in your debt. How is your superior, Mr. Hayden?"

"He got out of hospital in Philly yesterday. He's as tough as old boots and eager to get back into service."

Roosevelt nodded. "I'm glad to hear that. We need all the good people we can get right now." He patted a folder on the desk between them. "What about you? I hear your husband is a pilot flying bombers over Europe."

"Yes, Governor. I haven't seen him in months. We write as much as we can, but it was hard keeping in contact when I was running down the gang of Nazi saboteurs."

"More like impossible, I'd imagine. Your adopted country thanks you for your service and your sacrifice, but I'd like to help you out a little with that."

"You would, Governor?"

A sly smile came across the President's face. "It seems like the least I can do for saving my life. I was talking to our mutual friend Mr. Dulles, in Bern. He told me he snapped you up for service there."

"I'm looking forward to it."

"Well, how about stopping off in London to see your husband first? I know it's a little out of the way, but you deserve a little R&R before you launch back into the war."

Monika's heart bloomed. "That sounds wonderful, Governor."

"It's settled then. We need to look after our best people. And you're certainly one of them, Monika."

"Thank you!"

The aide walked over to the couch and gestured for Monika to rise.

"I'm sorry we have told the editors not to cover the story of your heroism in the newspapers, but with your profile, it wouldn't have been prudent to shout it from the rooftops, if you'll pardon the pun."

"Of course, Governor. I understand."

"But I won't forget about you. I want you to report to me personally whenever you're in Washington. And as soon as the war is won, I'll present you with the Presidential Medal of Freedom at the first opportunity. With all the pomp and circumstance you can imagine."

Roosevelt shook her hand again.

"Thank you, Governor."

"No. Thank *you*, Monika."

Though Monika walked out of the office alone she felt her parents' presence with every sinew of her being.

17

The Army Air Force base at Hardwick, England.

Michael walked into the interview room expecting the worst. The mission to Hamburg the previous day had been a disaster. Eight planes lost. 80 men captured or killed, and another dozen were in the hospital with burns, shrapnel, or gunshot wounds. Almost a third of the bombers sent out the day before hadn't come back. It was his fifth mission. The *Baby Doll* had survived with little more than a few bullet holes and a little shrapnel. Nothing had come close to what he'd experienced on his first sortie, but no one got lucky for long. Not here.

Michael's commanding officer, Colonel Bates, a sturdy man with a brown mustache and sallow skin, welcomed him into the bright room. It was a sunny April afternoon in England. The green fields outside seemed to glow in the afternoon light. Bates gestured for him to sit down. Michael did so with a curt nod.

"It was a tough day yesterday," the Colonel began.

"The flak was thicker than we'd anticipated," Michael said.

"The guns were hidden in the woods around the factory. We didn't see them until we were on top of them."

"Flying that low is always going to be dangerous," Bates answered. "It was a dangerous mission but that's why we got it. No one else could handle it. All your men okay?"

"Wallace, my tail gunner, caught a little shrapnel, but nothing too bad. He should be back in a week or so."

They spent the next 40 minutes going through the mission in intricate detail. They finished by going through what happened to each of the downed planes. Michael had seen three of them go down. They ended the meeting trying to ascertain who had died and who would spend the rest of the war in a German prisoner-of-war camp.

"You were friends with Captain Lewis, weren't you?" Bates asked.

Michael nodded. "He was a good man."

"Can you write his wife a letter? She just had a new baby a few months ago."

"I saw the photographs," Michael replied. "I'll do it today. If that's all, sir…" Michael said and rose from the chair.

"There's one more thing," Colonel Bates said. "This came right from the top. You've been ordered on a week's R&R beginning tomorrow."

"What? We're only five missions in. A lot of crews with three times as many haven't gotten any."

"Special orders. You and your entire bunch."

Michael didn't know how to feel. "Sir, I'm happy that my men will get a break, but I don't want to leave the rest of the squadron in the lurch."

"This order is from so far above my head that I'd have to get a stepladder to even see who sent it. Captain Ritter, this is an order. It doesn't matter how you or anyone else in this squadron feels about it."

"Thank you, sir."

"You're on specific orders to visit London. There's a train leaving in two hours. Tell your crew and pack your things."

Michael was puzzled. "Sir?"

"I have no idea, Ritter. I'm looking forward to finding out what's going on myself when you get back. In the meantime, just go and enjoy yourself. We'll be fine here without you."

Michael walked out of the interview room and scratched his head with a smile. He thought of Monika, as he always did in situations like this. She was the one he wanted to share this incredible news with. A letter to her would have to do. Her training over, she was in the process of being transferred to a diplomatic office in Switzerland. He hesitated in the hallway and reached for a worn photo of his wife he kept in his wallet. The angles of her face and the bright smile he cherished comforted him, and just for one moment, he was back at that party in Berlin in 1936 when he first laid eyes on her. He hadn't been able to resist her strength, her beauty, her vulnerability. He was in love in minutes.

The men of the *Baby Doll* stared at each other in disbelief as he broke the news to them. They reacted like him at first, but incredulity quickly turned to joy. Within a few seconds, they were hooting, hollering, and embracing one another. Judgements from others were dismissed.

Two hours later, Michael sat alone on the train to London. The other men had been taken to a rest facility in the Cotswolds, but for some reason he was set for something different. Theories abounded in his mind as he watched the English countryside flash past the train window. Most concerned his past in Germany and some possible use the OSS, or their British equivalent, the OSE, could have for him. He thought of the letters he'd written before leaving—one to his friend's wife, the other to his own. Perhaps one day one of his friends would write a letter to Monika to inform her of his last mission. It seemed more likely than not. He was no better a flyer than any of the men who'd gone down so far. Some were newbies, but many were experienced airmen who'd just run out of luck. No matter how good you were, luck was still key in surviving the clouds of deadly flak that greeted them in the skies over Europe. And things were only going to get more dangerous as the forays into Germany became more frequent.

Michael pondered his own death. He wondered if he'd done enough, seen enough, loved enough in his 25 years on this planet to leave something worthy behind. He tried to dismiss the specter of dying but it was impossible. Death was everywhere around him now. It was as much a part of his daily life as breathing or sleeping. Men died on every mission he flew. Sometimes from flak or enemy fighters but also from technical problems and basic failures of judgment. The instructors back in the States had tried to instill in them the level of peril they'd face as airmen, but few had believed them. Sure, many had died in training—more than he ever would have believed, but combat was a different animal. It was a vicious, snarling beast that had already devoured so many good men.

Michael stepped off the train at Waterloo Station among a large crowd. With rationing in place, the train was the only way for the public to travel long distances, and it seemed people were eager to leave the capital. A long line of women and children were waiting and eagerly piled onto the train as he walked away. A soldier at the end of the platform held up a sign. Michael laughed out loud as he saw it.

"You're here for me?" he said.

"Michael Ritter?" the man said in a thick Northern Irish accent. "Come with me."

The mystery was only deepening. "Where are we going?"

"You don't know?" the soldier asked with a smile. "We're off to the Ritz!"

"To meet whom, exactly?"

The Northern Irishman shook his head. "Now that I couldn't tell you!"

Michael sat in the back of the waiting car. He had been here once before, but only for a night, and had seen little other than the inside of a dance hall and several pubs.

It was a short drive over the river past Buckingham Palace to Mayfair, where the opulent Ritz Hotel sat untouched by the German bombs that had scarred much of the city around it.

"This is it," Michael's driver said as he pulled up outside.

"You're just dropping me off?"

The soldier smiled. "That's what I was ordered to do. Enjoy yourself with the toffs!"

Michael responded with a shrug of his shoulders and climbed out of the car. A man in a top hat and tails held the door for him. He stepped into a circular lobby with a plush red carpet under his feet. Uniformed doormen and bellboys buzzed around guests dressed as if they were about to attend a ball. With no idea where to go, Michael stopped a young bellboy and asked where the bar was. Two minutes later, Michael was sitting at the bar alone. He ordered a Scotch, even though beer would have been more to his taste.

Usually, he would have felt out of place in his Air Force uniform, but not during wartime.

"The first one's on the house," the bartender said.

Michael thanked him with a raised glass and sipped the expensive drink. He was starting to wonder if he'd be alone all afternoon when a voice from behind him lifted his soul.

"Since when did you drink whiskey?"

Michael whirled around to see his wife standing behind him, effortlessly beautiful in a blue sun dress and matching hat.

Unable to control himself, he lifted her in the air and kissed her. The feeling of her lips against his was unlike anything he'd ever known. It might have been 20 seconds or more before he put her down.

"What are you doing here? Did you organize this somehow?" he gasped.

Monika offered a knowing grin. "A friend in a high place asked me what I wanted. This is what I told him."

"You're here for a week? With me?"

Monika nodded, and he picked her up again.

"We're staying here. I just came from the room upstairs," she told him.

Once again, Michael felt like a husband, not just an Air Force pilot with nine other men's lives in his hands. It was good to realize there was still more to him than just that.

They sat at the bar for a few minutes before Monika led him upstairs to unpack.

They emerged from the room in time for dinner. After eating in the restaurant, they took a walk along Piccadilly and onto Regent Street. Busy shoppers milled past them on either side. Michael held his wife's hand as they went, unable to believe they were together. She'd almost become a mythical figure in his mind. The act of thinking about her so much had made her seem less real, more distant from his everyday life.

"Have you spoken to Mr. Dulles since you arrived in London?" he asked her.

"Not since I arrived here yesterday afternoon, but he's expecting me. He hasn't told me what I'm going to be doing but I'm eager to start. How have your missions been? You don't reveal much in your letters."

Michael hadn't told her about all his friends who'd died. He didn't want to sully this golden moment but answered her question anyway. "I've seen a lot of men die. No one in my plane so far. We've been lucky."

Monika didn't answer for a few seconds. Her voice was soft when she did. "How many men in your squadron?"

Michael shook his head. "Over 200. It's hard to know how many the Germans are holding. It can take a while for letters to get through once they're interned in the prisoner-of-war camps."

"What are the camps like?" she asked.

"I don't intend to find out," he replied with a weak smile. "I just want to do my 25 missions, come home, and sell war bonds."

"You have the face for it!" she grinned.

"What about you, Monika? Where's the end for you? Is there a tour of duty?"

She shook her head. "When the job's done, I suppose." They walked on a few yards, ignoring the ornate shop windows they passed. "Just promise me something."

"What?"

"When all this is over come back to me the same man you are now, the same boy I met at Goebbels' party in '36 who saved my life."

Michael saw the flak burst before his eyes, saw the heavy bombers spiraling to the earth in balls of flame and smoke, and then looked into his wife's eyes.

"I have no idea what you see, just where you'll be stationed. What about you? Can you stay the same?"

Monika squeezed his hand. "I don't know. Sometimes I think this war is going to change everyone it touches. I just hope that there's enough of who we were before it started left when it's over. We're fighting monsters. It's up to us to make sure we don't become them ourselves."

"Sometimes I think about those bombs we drop. With flak bursting around us and enemy fighters all over the skies, accidents happen. We've hit civilian areas. I know we have. I never see the faces of the people I kill, and I'll never know how many, but..."

Monika's lips tightened. "What's the alternative? We let the Nazis win? There's only one group of people responsible for those civilian deaths, and that's Hitler and his cronies themselves. The Germans are my people, but the real patriots are those who question the government and its motives, not those who blindly accept what the propagandists feed them every day. It's strange, but the best thing I can do for my country is to fight against it."

"You'll be recognized for what you do, and what you've sacrificed, someday."

"Recognition isn't my goal. I just want Germany to be free again."

They walked on a few more steps. A British soldier walked past with a young woman. She had one arm around him and was resting her head on his shoulder.

"I don't think any of us were ready for these times, though. Sometimes it seems like more than I can process," Michael said. "I'm terrified all the time."

"Yet, you still do it."

"I can't let the other men down."

"I feel exactly the same way."

The harsh sound of an air raid siren pierced the air. "It was too perfect," Michael said with a wry smile. People began to scatter for cover. A nearby policeman directed them to an air raid shelter, and they crowded in with the other evening shoppers, huddled together in Oxford Circus Tube station.

The sound of the bombs came. First as a whistling, then as a distant thud. The fire engines and ambulances followed in their wake. Michael pictured the night sky above London, alive with German bombers and British artillery fire. He pictured the flashlights piercing the night like massive golden sabers in the darkness. He pulled Monika closer, looked into her eyes, and found all the strength he'd ever need.

The End

A NOTE TO THE READER

I hope you enjoyed my book. Head over to www.eoindempseybooks.com to sign up for my readers' club. It's free and always will be. If you want to get in touch with me send an email to eoin@eoindempseybooks.com. I love hearing from readers so don't be a stranger!

Reviews are life-blood to authors these days. If you enjoyed the book and can spare a minute please leave a review on Amazon and/or Goodreads. My loyal and committed readers have put me where I am today. Their honest reviews have brought my books to the attention of other readers. I'd be eternally grateful if you could leave a review. It can be short as you like.

ALSO BY EOIN DEMPSEY

Standalones

Finding Rebecca

The Bogside Boys

White Rose, Black Forest

Toward the Midnight Sun

The Longest Echo

The Hidden Soldier

The Lion's Den Series (The first Ritter series)

1. The Lion's Den
2. A New Dawn
3. The Golden Age
4. The Grand Illusion
5. The Coming Storm
6. The Reckoning

The Maureen Ritter Series (The second Ritter series)

1. The American Girl
2. The Forger
3. The Secret Soldier

The Powerscourt Series

1. The Saint of Impossible Causes
2. The Garden of Ireland

ACKNOWLEDGMENTS

Writing this book was made all the easier by all the wonderful people who helped me along the way. Firstly, massive thanks again to the patron saints of this book, Carol McDuell, Cindy Bonner, and Michaelle Schulten. I can't thank you wonderful ladies enough. Also, to Maria Reid, Richard Schwarz, Frank Callahan, Ave Jeanne Ventresca, Cynthia Sand, Vickie Martin and Donna Greenberg, who went above and beyond.

As always, much love and gratitude to my mother, sister, Orla and my brothers Brian and Conor. And of course, my gorgeous wife, Jill and my three boys, Robbie, Sam, and Jack.

PRAISE FOR EOIN DEMPSEY

Praise for *The Hidden Soldier*:

"A heartfelt trip into two entangled time periods that fans will want to read in one sitting. Engrossing and surprising at every turn, the book is yet more proof that Dempsey is a master of the historical fiction genre."

— *LYDIA KANG, BESTSELLING AUTHOR OF A BEAUTIFUL POISON AND OPIUM AND ABSINTHE*

"The Hidden Soldier is a poignant page-turner that will leave you breathless. Gorgeously written, Eoin Dempsey carries you back in time and inserts you into the heart of this tragic, pivotal moment in history. Part thriller, part love story, I was completely enthralled from beginning to end."

— *SUZANNE REDFEARN, #1 AMAZON BESTSELLING AUTHOR OR IN AN INSTANT AND HADLEY AND GRACE.*

"'I didn't see that coming! Or that!" I yelled across the house as Eoin Dempsey's wonderful World War II book raced to an utterly satisfying wallop of a finale. His spare, dialogue-driven style, matched with his strong knowledge of the war and masterful ability to dance between two time periods, made for one heck of an enjoyable read."

— BOO WALKER, BESTSELLING AUTHOR OF AN UNFINISHED STORY.

Praise for *The Longest Echo*:

"...a chilling page turner that explores a shocking, little-known episode in history and manages to include a touching love story."

— HISTORICAL NOVEL SOCIETY

"A beautiful, heart wrenching novel that captivated me from the very beginning. This is historical fiction at its absolute best, and one of my favorite reads of the year."

— SORAYA M. LANE, AMAZON CHARTS BESTSELLING AUTHOR OF *WIVES OF WAR* AND *THE LAST CORRESPONDENT*

"Based on the true horrors of WWII Monte Sole, this story tugs at the heartstrings while delivering authentic, engaging champions and page-turning scenes that continue beyond the war."

— GEMMA LIVIERO, BESTSELLING AUTHOR OF HISTORICAL FICTION

Praise for *White Rose, Black Forest* (A Goodreads Choice Award Semifinalist, Historical Fiction):

"*White Rose, Black Forest* is partly a lyrical poem, an uncomfortable history lesson, and a page-turning thriller that will keep the reader engaged from the beginning to the end."

— FLORA J. SOLOMON, AUTHOR OF *A PLEDGE OF SILENCE*

"There is much to praise in Eoin Dempsey's *White Rose, Black Forest*, but for me it stands out from the glut of war fiction because of its poetic simplicity. The novel does not span a massive cast of characters, various continents, and the entire duration of the conflict. It is the tale of one young man, one young woman, and the courage to change the tide of a war. Emotional, taut, and deftly drawn, *White Rose, Black Forest* is a stunning tale of bravery, compassion, and love."

— AIMIE K. RUNYAN, BESTSELLING AUTHOR OF *DAUGHTERS OF THE NIGHT SKY*

"Dempsey's World War II thriller is a haunting page-turner. The settings are detailed and the characters leap off the page. I couldn't put this book down. An instant bestseller."

— JAMES D. SHIPMAN, BESTSELLING AUTHOR OF *IT IS WELL* AND *A BITTER RAIN*

"A gripping story of heroism and redemption, *White Rose, Black Forest* glows with delicate yet vivid writing. I enjoyed it tremendously."

— OLIVIA HAWKER, AUTHOR OF *THE RAGGED EDGE OF NIGHT*

"Tense, taut, and tightly focused, *White Rose, Black Forest* is a haunting novel about courage and compassion that will keep you gripped from the very first page."

— COLIN FALCONER, BESTSELLING AUTHOR OF *THE UNKILLABLE KITTY O'KANE*

ABOUT THE AUTHOR

Eoin (Owen) was born and raised in Ireland. His books have been translated into fourteen languages and also optioned for film and radio broadcast. He lives in Philadelphia with his wonderful wife and three crazy sons.

You can connect with him at eoindempseybooks.com or on Facebook at https://www.facebook.com/eoindempseybooks/ or by email at eoin@eoindempseybooks.com.

Printed in Great Britain
by Amazon